JAYDEE HOFFER
WRITER/CREATOR

GABO IBARRA
ILLUSTRATOR

ALFONSO RUIZ
ILLUSTRATOR

KOTE CARVAJAL
COLORS

MAX BERTOLINI
ALTERNATE COVER/
COLORS

-Lord Melech-

(Ruler of Argoss)

"Scylus is excited to see
what you're capable of...
and so am I."

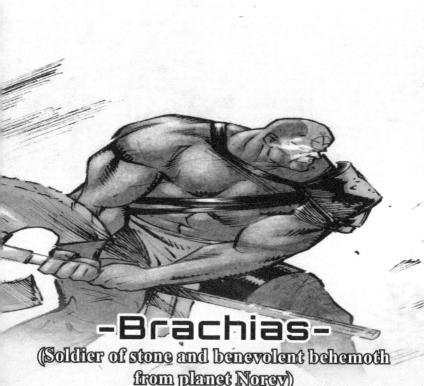

-Brachias-
(Soldier of stone and benevolent behemoth from planet Norev)

We fight for our king.
And we die for our country.
Let our reasons be understood.
And our sacrifices noted.
(Spartan Oath)

SPARTANS IN SPACE

Jaydee Hoffer

Gabo Ibarra

Alfonso Ruiz

Kote Carvajal

Max Bertolini

"The most valiant are sometimes
the most unfortunate.
Thus there are triumphant defeats that rival
victories."
-Michel De Montaigne-

1

In the year 18,085 humans no longer inhabit the earth...
Centuries of war and civil dissatisfaction had pitted man
against himself in a desperate rush to eliminate competition and secure the last of the planet's remaining natural
resources for himself, made scarce through a global pan-
demic of overpopulation and scrupulous self-indulgence...
In the end, no price was too great, and man eventually
destroyed himself, wiping himself and all life off the face
of the earth, forever...
The rise and fall of man went virtually unnoticed, and no
other life has ever stepped foot on the earth since.
Until now...

SPARTANS IN SPACE 01

A lone starship approaches...
As it makes its way towards the earth, it slows down and
takes position moving steadily along the upper part of the
atmosphere...
From here you can spot details of Earth, and prying eyes
lay sights on them for the very first time...
Eerily appearing beyond the first ship, a large collection
of lights gradually reveal themselves as the rest of a massive fleet...
Joining the first ship, the vast battalion floats ominously
high above the surface of the planet...
Looking out from inside the ships, an array of varied
shaped silhouettes take in the scenery as the monochrome
landscape greets them all with the husk of a beautiful city
standing dry and deserted...
A veritable desert, skyscrapers that once seemingly stood
tall now stand pathetically reaching upwards as if desperately begging someone above to come down there and
save them...
Complex roads with no apparent beginning or end now
wind congested with foul mounds of litter and outdated
machinery.
As the ships steadily hover, four large towers located
just under the front of one start to converge towards each
other.
Slowly easing their way forward, the towers
Shift sixty degrees. Ceasing, with the end of each tower
meeting the other, the four surround an invisible center,
generating a noxious, luminous, teal steam.
The towers suddenly begin gathering energy.
The steam is quick to fade, as just in that instant, a massive beam bursts forth from between the four towers and
is instantly sent screaming towards a neighboring
mountainside...

CRASH!!!...

The beam slams into the rockface, tearing a hole into it as it divides into a million bolts of energy that rise like vines from the hole and grow in every direction...

The barren Earth is blanketed, taken over by the blue-ish-green, meandering light spreading out throughout the world now like a complex system of veins.

As each bolt begins to harden, it becomes a perpetual 360-degree lens capable of gazing at the planet now from any direction.

As fields of these translucent tendrils infect the earth, wrapping themselves around skyscrapers and trees, per-meating the subterranean underpasses of empty subway stations, each one suddenly begins to emit a faint, lumi-nous pulse...

Amidst the harmonious silence and ominous wind all you can hear are the faint droning sounds now coming from all of them.

The tendrils capture images of the despoiled planet.

Harnessing data, the tendrils begin sending vast amounts of information back now to the leading starship.

Inside the ship...

In a room where the only light comes from buttons spread across countless control panels, a small band of shady characters, each unique to their own species, gather in front of a large monitor screen.

As images of a dry, desolate Earth make their way onto the screen, all but one of the beings suddenly break into a cacophonous state of worrisome chit chat and banter.

Studying the images, as the one stands firm looking up at the screen, face hidden by shadows from the dimly lit chamber, he suddenly turns his head towards the tumultuous bunch, and with regards to the ship, he gives an order he expects to be carried out right away...

"Take her down..."

Ship touches earth, and boots touch sand as the one makes his way down the large cargo ramp on the back of the ship.

His name is Scylus...

Trailing behind, a unit of four soldiers run past, stopping just beyond the foot of the ramp.

Each one, a son from his own planet stands firm, lightly armed, waiting to be acknowledged by the olive-toned honcho now firmly approaching...

"Captain Scylus!" they shout, giving their salute to the one distinguishable by the dark-purple cloak draped over the brushed, carbon black and gray breastplate.

Scylus assesses his surroundings.

Slowly turning his head from left to right, Scylus grabs a quick overview of the

wilderness around him...

He finds himself standing in a world of rocks and sand littered thick with debris from the ruins of the once familiar cities to the now extinct humans...

Scylus squints as he scopes, before looking back at the four soldiers standing fixed, firmly awaiting their orders...

"Scan the perimeter," he says.

"Explore the surrounding terrain.

Check the area and report back to me any signs of life you might find."

"Sir!" the four confirm, flashing their salute before dividing off to explore in their own direction...

Scylus watches them off...

Contemplating alone in the harsh, sharp wind, Scylus looks down and notices something in the sand that suddenly grabs his attention.

"..?"

Down by his boots, lying partially buried by the side of a mangled up license plate, is the tattered top corner of the

spine from an old book.

"Hmm..."

Scylus lowers himself to reach for the book.

Grabbing hold of it, Scylus lifts it up close to inspect it.

The book is a faded black...

Aided by a device embedded in his head, Scylus is able to render the text on the face decipherable.

The cover reads—

Magnus Compendium: Analytical Works and Military Texts From Around The Ancient World.

The cover features a broad man in a red cape, holding a sword, standing formidable, wearing a fearsome looking helmet.

Inside the book, Scylus confronts dated ideological texts and stories of ancient clashes of shield and sword time had seemingly discarded...

Reading through the book at an incredible pace, Scylus's eyes flash hot-white as he absorbs the information.

Perusing through parts of a page, the olive-toned honcho suddenly stops at a section that peaks his interest.

Narrowing his eyes, Scylus dives into its contents.

Picking apart the text on a section of bottom page, Scylus inadvertently stumbles onto a recount of the tale of *The 300.*

The section states—

Clouds move with the multitude, and the ground shakes with the million or so
foreign invaders making their way towards the grounds of Thermopylae.
From the east, three-hundred Greeks from the city of Sparta and their king head off to face them in an epic

battle that will come to forever echo within the confines of history.

Scylus reads on, learning about the three days the three-hundred Spartans would hold their own against an army massing over a hundred times their size.
Pages paint an elite warrior culture structured around strict discipline and selective practices meant to separate weak children from fit, ensuring only the strongest Spartans would survive to grow up and become warriors.
"Fascinating..."

With everything Scylus has read, he suddenly finds himself looking out at the sand blasted Earth.
Clutching the book at his side, Scylus looks down at it when,
suddenly,
he gets an idea...

A handful of Spartans were mentioned during details of the battle, but not so much as one who stood out from the rest. One who garnered esteem and was regularly exalted above all others—Leonidas...
The book says that Leonidas died fighting alongside his men, and that the Spartan king's bones were later recovered and buried inside a commemorative tomb maintained throughout modern day Greece.
The remains of The 300 were all buried in the same place where they made their last stand on the grounds of Thermopylae...

Impressed by the story, a cold smirk paints itself across Sylus's face as he pictures a team of Spartan elites raiding garrisons and living a life devoted exclusively to selfless duty to Lord Melech.

Lord Melech...
The charismatic, self appointed grandmaster of all,
Melech won't stop until all life in the universe bows
down before him: acknowledging him as their wonderful
supreme leader, and ultimate perfect being...

2

Hailing from the wasteland supercities of planet Argoss,
Lord Melech sends emissaries like Scylus off into space,
looking for distant planets to overcome and subjugate
their populaces.
Melech then adds them to the sum of other planets that all
make up the vast
majority of his Argoss empire...
Hundreds of thousands of infants are taken annually and
reared on Argoss, where they are trained and brought up
as soldiers or ship personnel, offering them the
opportunity to serve in the budding regime...

Lost in thought, Scylus fails to notice the return of the four soldiers...

"Captain Scylus!" one says, drawing Scylus's attention.
"We've finished scouring the perimeter, sir.
No signs of life anywhere..."
Scylus looks at the four with condescending muse before smiling and speaking to them, looking down at the book.
"Hmm... Can't enslave a people without people to enslave now can we?
Ha-ha!"
Scylus raises the book up and shows it to them.
"No matter...
I think we've got something we can use...
Back to the ship!"

Back on board, crewmen receive word from Scylus to ready the ship for take-off.
Buttons are pressed, and knobs are rendered as the ship wails a thick, high pitched mechanical sound.
Vents open releasing pressurized fumes, blowing tons of sand up from the ground in every direction.
Scylus and his men are more than halfway up the ramp when it slowly begins to rise...
Inside the ship, Scylus enters the bridge; the room is electric with activity.
Crewmen from all planets hustle about tending to monitors and terminals as buttons throughout flicker in harmonious light patterns...
Scylus takes his seat down on the captains' chair, at the heart of the commotion.
Stone-faced, poised, and unsettlingly calm, Scylus resembles a medieval judge ready to cite law and cast his verdict out to all those awaiting conviction.

"Activate propulsion systems," he orders.
"Initiate thrust drives and bring images from the outside up onto the screen!"
With that, thrusters outside the ship engage, releasing a propulsion energy so hot it turns the sand around it to glass.
The ship gradually lifts as internal reactors combust and launch its body skyward...
As the ship gains altitude, a video feed from outside is rendered and transmitted over the large central monitor at the front of the bridge.

Details from the ground dwindle as the ship climbs higher and higher and higher until gravity gives, thrusters cease, and the ship sits silently adrift in low orbit.
All is quiet onboard.
".......

Sitting in his chair, Scylus quietly contemplates something.
Affecting the general silence on the ship with his own silence, the crew watches as Scylus dissociates completely from them, pondering perfectly stoic...
Minutes pass, and one of Scylus's subordinates finally approaches him.
"C-Captain Scylus?"
"....."
Unaffected by the verbal nudge subtly lunged by his subordinate, Scylus maintaines his train of thought, crossing one leg over the other, nullfully brushing the crewman off.
"S-Standing by to await orders, sir..."
The subordinate's body starts rattling nervously.

Scylus turns to take a look at the visibly intimidated officer...

"Bring me the machine..."

The officer stiffens and turns without a word before he swiftly begins making his way off of the bridge.

The doors on the bridge part as the officer departs, before they just as quickly close, sealing the entrance behind him.

As Scylus waits for the officer to return, he grabs his recently acquired book and casually walks it over to the large central monitor at the front of the bridge.

The monitor shows the ship now hovering over what was once central Europe, and Scylus enters a series of button combinations into a console just a few feet from the front of the monitor screen.

A small circular hatch on the console suddenly slides open, and a luminescent mist of neon green with thin swirls of yellow light slowly rises from the hatch like a mix of electricity and fog coming from the depths of the machine.

Scylus sets the book over the small opening of the hatch. The science of the light keeps the book floating in place, tossing and turning like a small box caught in an updraft. Streaks of yellow light phase through the book, scanning its contents and collecting all the information stored within its pages...

Sometime later,
doors on the bridge *CHSHH!* as they suddenly slide open.
Scylus has his back facing the doors and initially doesn't notice the return of his subordinate.

"Captain Scylus!" the officer calls out.
Scylus turns around to look at the officer and finds him

standing behind him along with four guards carrying a large, metallic, cylindrical device...

The metalwork on the device is solid black, and all neo tech, cutting edge, with illuminated slits of color permeating throughout.

Its radiance is of a cold mechanical beauty.

Within the visible core of the cylinder sits the Xarcon Gem, a dark-purple and black crystal that pulsates violently from within a transparent central chamber.

"The Xarcon Cylinder, as you requested, captain," the officer says.

Scylus takes a moment to look at The Cylinder—then looks up at the five.

"Cast it down to the designated gunport on the ship's lower level," he says.

"Have crew there sync it to one of the modified hull cannons and tell them to stand by, afterwards, and wait for my orders."

"Sir!"

the five confirm,

and they turn around and begin making their way off of the bridge...

As the five head out, the one officer looks back hoping to catch a word with Scylus before taking off.

The four guards continue out, hauling the device...

Standing at the edge of the doorway, the officer looks on, staring inquisitively at Scylus.

Studying the honcho, the officer takes a moment to grab gumption before finally speaking.

"What do you plan to do?..."

Scylus smiles as he looks on at the timid officer.

"I plan to tell fate it was wrong..."

SPARTANS IN SPACE 01

Not sure what he means by the vague remark, the officer
opts to not risk a vicious reprimand brought about by
questions abound, and irritating Scylus.
He doesn't say another word.
The officer quietly excuses himself,
and makes his way off the bridge,
with both doors sliding closed steadily behind him.
Scylus turns back towards the console and looks up at the
screen, where the remains of Leonidas and his 300 lay
highlighted with coordinates on a video feed of modern
day Greece...
Excerpts from the book reveal their locations, and cosmic
calculations from the onboard computers determine their
whereabouts...
Pages from the book later confirm Leonidas's bones were
later taken to what are now the ruins of the National Museum of Science and History, in the neo city of Rhodes.
Scylus decides to start there...

Using images taken by the system of light tendrils now
scattered across the earth, Scylus is able to locate the
exact whereabouts of the museum.

Meanwhile...

Down in the depths of below deck, inside of a long dimly lit chamber where the ship's hull cannons retract to when not being engaged, crew there receive the Xarcon Cylinder from the officer and four guards...

Among the dozens of cannons lined up on both sides of the walls, workers have updated and modified three to use in conjunction with the Xarcon Cylinder...

The crew slides the cylinder in through the cannon barrel, locking it in place.

KACHNK!

Up on the bridge, Scylus stands quietly transfixed to the large monitor screen.

All he can think about are the numerous ways he plans to exploit the Spartans once they're successfully resurrected...

3

Crew on the bridge steadily busy themselves punching in coordinates on their terminals, simultaneously feeding them to the modified hull cannon below deck.

Coordinates are sent and messages are relayed back to the crewmen up on the bridge.

"Captain Scylus!" one says.

"Modifications have been completed, sir!

The Cylinder has been integrated and the target coordinates are fully innate within it!"

"Excellent!" Scylus says.

"Initiate the ready sequence!..."

SPARTANS IN SPACE 01

Hull cannons gather in energy as the ship breaks orbit and jettisons back into Earth...
Inside the ship, intel from the book, plus scans of the planet yield comprehensive data that guides Scylus and the ship steadily towards the ruins of the sidecast museum...

Flying over the pacific, the water reflects the light from the Earth's gluttoned sun as mutated creatures reminiscent of dolphins breach to breathe before disappearing again just as quickly into the altered depths.
The ship turns left...

Minutes turn to miles and miles lead to land as the ship finally finds itself flying over central Greece...

Like a large storm cloud casting its shadow, the ship closes in on the torn remnants of the museum.

The neo city of Rhodes, like all cities on Earth, stands eroded,
distorted,
a dead leaf whose whole exists with holes, and who's long been stripped of the green from its former glory.
"Zoom in on the target museum!" Scylus orders.
Cameras outside the ship zoom in as details from the area gradually grow clearer and clearer...

On an open stretch of land surrounded by rocks and the barely discernible bases of the buildings that once stood there, stand the battered remnants of Greece's National Museum of Science and History...

"Send scouts to go in and find what we're looking for,"

Scylus orders,
and the massive cargo hatch on the back of the ship partially drops and hangs open.

A dry gust bellows across the museum grounds as three dots swirl out from the ship's open cargo hatch just above it.

Three scouts rain down in jetpack and uniform, lightly armed, with special wrist coms fitted to communicate with Scylus.

Landing only meters away from the once-was museum, the three scouts, a team of lean reptilian beings, head forward henceforth eager to please their olive-toned honcho.

Entering the building with weapons drawn, the three take point, having one watch over the other as they ease their way in...

Inside, a filthy amalgamation of relics, junk and debris lays scattered across the former main hall of the museum. Most of the exhibits inside are either destroyed or blocked off by large chunks of building that had gradually corroded and broken away...

The three aren't even halfway into the building when a bright blue light suddenly rises and spreads out over the tops of their wrist coms.

A three dimensional image of Scylus is suddenly presiding over each of them.

"I want you three to find—this," it says, showing the image of a long rectangular glass case exhibited on one of the pages of the Magnus Compendium.

Inside the glass case, fragments of fossilized bone on top of folded crimson cloth: the fossilized remains of Leonidas ripe with potential to convert and reanimate...

The three scouts look all over sections of the museum before they finally spot the bones littered amongst trash and remnants of building...

SPARTANS IN SPACE 01

The glass case the bones had been housed in had been smashed, leaving only fragments and miniscule samples lying amongst tatters of crimson shreds.
One of the scouts gathers the pieces inside a net composed entirely of orange light as another motions for the other two to follow him as he makes his way back towards the entrance.
The three holler and cheer from the success of their mission, kicking up dust and debris as they excitedly run through the bits and pieces of countless other exhibits.
"Woo-hoo!
Mission accomplished," one of them says.
Less than fifty feet from where the museum doors would be, the three scouts turn on their jetpacks and storm wildly out of the building, jettisoning upwards towards the ship in a colorful spiral formation...

Once inside, the three scouts kneel, presenting their findings to Scylus.
Scylus, very stoically, grabs the net and hands it off to a little blue alien standing off to one side.
Timid, and dressed in white, the little alien's coat carries the symbol of all those who practice science on Argoss.
"You know what to do," Scylus says, looking at the alien.
The little alien begins to make his way off the bridge.
He is more than halfway to the doors when Scylus suddenly calls after him.
"Hmmff! oh, and, Cerix..."
"...?!"
The little blue alien looks back.
"Don't disappoint me..."
"Y-Yessir..."
Cerix lowers his head and walks off, turning a corner beyond the bridge doors before disappearing from sight.

Meanwhile...

"Set a new course!" Scylus orders.
"Continue to the next destination point and stand by with the modified hull cannon..."
The crewmen set course, setting their sights west from the neo city of Rhodes to the ancient grounds of Thermopylae, where The 300 fell.

A short time later...
Down in the cavernous sublevels of the ship, in a subsection dedicated to science and nooks of the arcane, Cerix walks quietly down a long, dark hallway...
On both sides of the hall are labs running down it, each filled with other scientists the same race as his...
In the labs, the scientists all gather, forced to set and carry out all kinds of scientific experiments...
As Cerix makes his way over towards one end of the hall, he stops in front of a massive gunmetal door.
The door slides open, and Cerix walks through, entering a colossal lab the size of an aircraft hangar.
Inside, two scientists too busy to notice Cerix, mindfully carry out their duties...
While one scientist tinkers with machinery high above the floor, the other casually walks the lab, reading spreadsheets out loud to himself...
Occupying one end of the lab are two steel, gray, colossal towers.
Between the two towers, a large, abrasive, sandy-beige diamond parabolically hangs from a black metal mounting attached to a forest of tangled red, and mustard cables.
Thirty feet below the diamond, a large collection of iridescent electrical columns and high-tech machinery.

The two towers stand like large metallic scarecrows amidst a colorful electric garden.

Cerix walks to a nearby terminal.

Punching in a sequence of numbers and symbols, Cerix pours the fossils into a nearby receptacle intrinsically linked to the rough, hanging diamond and large circular platform...

One of the scientists notices Cerix and suddenly approaches him.

"What are you doing?" the scientist says, concerned.

"Scylus wants these samples put through the Transmutation Matrix right away," Cerix replies.

The scientist pauses, looking at the empty, pulsating net in Cerix's hand.

"Does he even know what these samples are from?"

"He has some *idea*, apparently," Cerix responds.

"And he plans on reviving three-hundred more after this..."

Outside...

The ship slowly crosses between Thebes and New-Athens, gradually casting its black shadow over the grounds of Thermopylae.

Inside the ship,

"What are our current coordinates?!" Scylus asks, as the hull cannons engage, slowly emerging from the bottom of the ship.

"Readings confirm we are just over the destination point!" a crewman calls out. "Modified hull cannon has been deployed and is currently standing by, captain!"

"Good...

Commence with a comprehensive terra scan of the terrain."

The ship scans a section of earth, revealing a large collection of fossilized remains centralized around the grounds of Thermopylae...

Tech onboard discerns the fossils from anything else, and confirms the remains of The 300 from Sparta.

Back in the lab, Cerix listens to the ravings of a hysterical Scientist...

"I mean, it's virtually untested!...

We don't even know if the Transmutation Matrix can reanimate one, let alone three-hundred!

What is Scylus thinking?!.."

"It would seem," Cerix says, "Scylus has other plans..."

"It was raw luck Argoss found the stones when they did!" the scientist continues.

"What are the odds two receptive Xarconian Gems would just be floating out here in space eight years after planet Xarcanose was blasted into fragments?!"

"I *could* do the math," Cerix replies, "But I'm pretty sure you were just being rhetorical."

"*(Sigh)*

Unanimous planetary suicide—

A novel, archaic practice.

In any case, the crystal inside the cylinder is too unstable to be overworked.

If Scylus crosses that threshold th-"

"Maybe Scylus knows something we don't," Cerix interrupts dispassionately.

The concerned scientist continues.

"The stones react when in proximity to each other, generating *huge* amounts of energy.

If that connection gets severed the other stone loses its charge and is eventually rendered useless within a matter of hours...

I just hope Scylus knows what he's doing..."

Outside the ship, the modified hull cannon locks onto its designated section of earth on the grounds of Thermopy-lae...
Tension peaks as Scylus waits for confirmation, to give the order.

"Confirmation received, sir!" one officer calls out.
"We have target lock on the designated grounds!"
"Excellent..."

It was no more than a whisper, really—
Lost in the wake, Scylus knew he would be challenging fate with a word...

"Fire."

A concussive blast of dark-purple and white energy suddenly bursts out from the end of the modified hull cannon...

A beam of light whizzes through the air, shaking the ground as it touches down.

The beam maintains a constant stream while preserving the integrity of the soil, a side effect from the hill cannon's beam being filtered through the gem set in the core of the Xarcon Cylinder.

The beam charges the ground, lacing it with its energy signature.

The fossils below begin glowing an unnatural violet.

Inside the ship, Scylus orders personnel to siphon off a portion of the beam's energy.

"I want a ten percent cutback rerouted!" he says.

"Have it shifted down to the lab housing the Transmutation Matrix.

Have our scientists initiate the re-an sequence with the samples recovered from the museum..."

Buttons are pressed, the beam outside blinks, and looks a fraction thinner by the end of a split second.

Energies are rerouted to the lab where Cerix is busy running diagnostic tests on Leonidas's remains...

It only takes moments for a special system of pipes along the ceiling of the lab to glow as the irradiated stream of violet energy begins to run through them.

Down a maze of specialized ducts, the energy is run through the receptacle holding Leonidas's bones, before it's recast and shot through the rough, sandy beige diamond hanging between the two towers...

The diamond reacts after being exposed, awakening the properties within it that gather around it and glow like moths to a light.

On one side of the lab, the bones are doused with the beam's energy, as monitors around them suddenly spring and come to life revealing codes and symbols laying out the genetic composition and inner workings of the fossilized remains...

4

Cerix walks over to a nearby console.

Pressing a button, Cerix initiates the reanimation sequence.

Just a few feet away, the circular platform begins to resonate, as the two towers release a hailstorm of loud, deep mechanical sounds.

"Ready..." Cerix joylessly declares.

The diamond above the platform glows hot-white.

Information is processed and the machine begins altering the fossil's physiology, piecing together the missing parts of the Spartan's genetic code...

Concentric rings of sky-blue light materialize and expand over the platform before disappearing again.

and again in a continuous loop.

Anticipation swells in the lab as piece by piece, and cell by cell, machines argue with fate to steal a body back.

KRIK-CLASHHH !!!

A small electrical storm unfurls over the platform as the air in the lab rumbles and countless machines shake!

Not long after, the electrical storm settles before collapsing into itself, breaking down to a singularity and expanding again as a vertical line segment with an ethereal glow. As the line segment slowly lowers itself onto the platform, it spreads out and begins to take on the shape of a broad man looking down, kneeling...

Back on the bridge,

Scylus watches as crewmen run around hysterically, checking monitors, analyzing data, concerned with keeping the overall integrity of the beam sicced onto the earth...

From the ship, Scylus looks out at the dust bowl planet. Looking back at the bustling crew, he orders a status update on the remnants of The 300.

"What's the word on our three-hundred friends, hmm?"

"All remnants in the soil have been doused and registered, sir." one officer declares. "Physiological data has been captured and is on its way to the lab for reanimatio-"

CHZRKKT!

"The specimen has escaped!!!"

The frantic words from an unnerved Cerix suddenly blare into the bridge, along with his image, as a video feed of him in the lab with the other two scientists is suddenly brought up in front of all, on the large monitor screen.

Cerix's worrisome eyes do little to hide his fear as behind him the two other scientists run back and forth frantically in and out of frame.

Scylus looks up at the monitor with a cold, vicious scowl. "Whaaat...?"

The green honcho's brows gradually furrow.

"What!

Happened?!"

Cerix's tiny fist clench as he grabs the cloth of his jacket. "H-He just—left!

A team of guards came in to check on us, and as soon as they did, the subject saw that the door was open and he seized the opportunity.

Ran through the guards like they were nothing!

He could be hiding anywhere now..."

An angry look paints itself across Scylus's face before recovering and brushing it off just as quickly.

"Hmmf! No matter...

Stand by for fossil data on the remaining three-hundred Spartans.

Initiate the reanimation sequence when ready.

I'll send another team of guards down there to assist you in a moment."

Scylus cuts the call short and turns to the crew manning the terminals when,

just then—

BOOOM!!!

One of the monitors from a nearby terminal suddenly explodes spraying an amalgamation of smoke, glass, and electrical parts at an unsuspecting Scylus.

"Argh!"

Scylus raises his arm up to cover his face and protect himself from the flash of debris.

Looking up from his arm and down at the monitor, Scylus sees a gaping hole lined with severed wires sparking at the tip from a spot on a terminal where a monitor used to be.

Scylus looks back at the crew suddenly, raging, confused. "What! happened?!"

"Xarcon Cylinder radiation levels have spiked, sir!" an anxious crew member reports.

"Structural integrity within the crystal's core has plummeted.

It's lashing out against itself!"

Outside the ship, from inside the modified hull cannon, the Xarcon Cylinder shakes as the central gem within it rages and raves in a violent display of blotches of black-burgundy, and violet light.

It only takes seconds for the gemstone to crack, releasing its energies and swallowing up the hull cannon in a bright vibrant explosion,

FWOOOOOOM!

Scylus and his men all feel the floor shake from under them...

"Find out what that was!" Scylus orders.

A handful of crew exude rejuvenated fervor in manning their terminals and ascertaining the origin of the rumbling they felt.

Running comprehensive diagnostic checks, crew scan the ship and search through all parts for any anomalies...

"Captain Scylus!" one crew member reports, "Modified hull cannon no longer registering on the monitor, sir!"

Scylus looks out again from inside the ship.

The violet beam that once saturated the ground is no

longer in sight.

Off to the side, towards the lower front end of the ship, Scylus spots large sparks shooting outwards in short repetitive bursts.

Scylus looks to one side and sighs.

"Dam..."

Scylus takes a moment to gather his thoughts when—

"We have multiple reports coming in from various sources inside the ship!" one crewman shouts out.

"Sources report being attacked by an unknown assailant while conducting their rounds.

No deaths have been reported, although several members of security *have* been seriously injured."

"It's him" Scylus utters to himself.

With that, Scylus quickly gathers himself and swiftly lays out orders for all of the crew.

"Seal all doors!" he voices.

"No one comes or goes without proper clearance!

"Gather a small tactical unit to go after the Spartan.

Assemble a larger group to head down to the sub-lab for support!

And arrange for a group of technicians to go ascertain the condition of the Xarcon Cylinder.

Have them salvage what they can..."

Orders are punched into machines by the crew on deck and sent out to personnel on all parts of the ship.

"Upload security feeds!" Scylus orders.

A large flat monitor slowly lowers itself down from the ceiling.

Showcasing a "chessboard" of smaller windows, the monitor shows the individual live footage throughout the ship.

As Scylus begins studying the feeds, squares on the chessboard suddenly start to go out.

CHZZKT!

"...?!"

One by one, footage goes blank as the terrified screams of frightened crewmen can be easily discerned amongst the audio.

"Captain Scylus!"

Some of them yell,

while others wail out a jumbled up hodgepodge of bundled up jargon,

"Uraghhhhohuhahhh!!!"

Scylus looks on at the screen, with a one wide-eyed silent expression,

his concentration cut short by the same pleads and screams now gradually making their way outside the bridge doors.

"Captain Scylus!!!"

A small commotion is heard and then—silence...

as the previously locked doors of the bridge now suddenly slide open...

5

In steps a tall, muscular man in the nude with long hair, dragging a barely conscious member of security in with him by the stretches of his uniform.

The man, standing three inches shorter than Scylus, looks up at the decorated ship captain; his beard barely concealing the arrogant grin across his face.

"So..." the man says.

"You must be Scylus."

The man drops the security guard.

"I kept hearing that name as I wandered over here. I'm really sorry about your friend there...

But it would seem like he could use some more training."

Amused by the brash confidence, Scylus lowers his head and smiles to himself—raising it up again just before looking back at the Spartan and promptly replying,
"Heh...
So it would seem..."
Scylus decides to indulge the Spartan.
"I'm impressed you managed to make it this far.
Tell me...
Do you even know where you are...?"
"Well!," Leonidas exclaims, grabbing his chin, smiling, with sharp eyes fixed on Scylus.
"Judging by the looks of you,
I'd say I must be in Hades...
Heh..."
"You're not in Hades," Scylus says.
"In fact, any place you might have thought of has long since gone and expired.
It is only by my grace that you are even standing here at all.
You have been given a second chance, Leonidas!...
Let me explain..."

Scylus brings Leonidas up to speed, explaining the nature of the Spartan's resurrection, while using double speech to mislead him and get him to cooperate...

"So you see, Leonidas!" Scylus explains.
"The universe is in great need of your assistance!...
Countless worlds have grown ignorant and weak and it is up to people like us to help save them from themselves...
Imagine it.
Directionless worlds without a proper leader to guide them.

They must be rehabilitated," Scylus assures.

"And, when necessary—conquered to ensure that they begin to see things for the way they really are..."

Leonidas stares at the tall, olive-toned being, studying him carefully...

"And why would I help you?" Leonidas retorts.

"Because, Leonidas..."

The expression on Scylus's face sharpens as his voice grows softer and head projects forward.

"I can give it all back to you..."

"Huh?!"

Scylus delights in the sudden igniting of the Spartan's emotions.

"Even as we speak, my scientists below are busy working on bringing your fallen comrades back to life.

How much sweeter then would it be to apply this technology in bringing back all those whom you never got the chance to see again?..."

Leonidas swallows hard and then blinks, barely able to grasp what Scylus has just said.

"I could resurrect your planet," Scylus declares, staring intensely at Leonidas...

"I could bring back the lush greenery, and give you a place to rule once more where you and those closest to you can *thrive* quietly.

I am offering you a second chance at life.

An existence free from resistance, and enmity from your enemies who've all long since been dead.

I can get Sparta back for you.

And all it would take,

is the unbridled allegiance from you and your men
throughout a short military stint as soldiers for Argoss of
only two full years.
After which then we will go back to your planet,
and I'll give you all everything you deserve when it's
time to part ways.
What do you say?..."
Leonidas closes his eyes and contemplates the offer...
In his mind, he sees images of the world he left behind.
He can feel the warmth of the breeze in the spring.
He can hear the swaying of the trees in the summer.
And every face that has ever meant anything to him
throughout his life suddenly comes back to him relent-
lessly in flashes repeating over and over...
The spartan is overwhelmed by a flood of emotion, feel-
ing everything he's ever felt for anyone at once...
With the terms Scylus claims under the deal he's put for-
ward a decision is made.
And Leonidas opens his eyes,
looks up at the olive-toned honcho and firmly replies...

"Take me to my men..."

6

Down below,
In the now bustling sub-lab housing the Transmutation
Matrix, a concert of cold smoke, lights, and security personnel oversee the dozens of little blue scientists working
frantically now trying to conserve the fleeting energy
from the diamond hanging between the two towers.
The diamond has been running on "fumes" now since the
destruction of the Xarcon Cylinder...

A tense ride down a long elevator shaft takes Leonidas
and Scylus down through the ship's mysterious
sub-levels.
Leonidas has since been given garments to wear: top and
bottoms made out of a strong, black, elastic material that
adjusts firmly to the user's body; cutting off just above
the ankles and shoulders...
The shoes Leonidas has on are made from a strong
composite material laid in a gray, black and white color
palette.
Small aesthetics line the chest and one side of the thigh,
displaying strange alien symbols Leonidas has never
seen...
Down the elevator shaft, Leonidas turns his head to look
at Scylus—only to find him staring back with a disturb-
ing, detached, silent expression...
It isn't long before both of them feel a slight *jerk*
from the elevator as it starts to slow down.

VMMMMMMMMCHSHHHH.....

Doors open,
and Leonidas and Scylus step out, finding themselves
looking down the stretch of a long cavernous hallway.
Dimly lit—save for the light coming from the dozens of
rooms lining both sides of it, Leonidas and Scylus both
eventually begin to make their way down the hallway...
Leonidas recalls these rooms during his initial escape,
and remembers the little blue aliens working inside them.
Of which there seems to be less of them now in them, he
notices.
The expression across the little blue aliens' faces are
painted vividly inside Leonidas's mind: Miserable...
Broken...

Stuck...

Struck with an utter sense of hopelessness that resonates in their motions and hovers around their white lab coats...

"This is the research hall," Scylus explains.

"No doubt you passed by here during your *daring escape*," he cites, mockingly.

"The little blue creatures you see there are Etherians. And they happily work themselves for the scientific advancement of Argoss and Lord Melech."

Leonidas says nothing.

As they approach the end of the hallway, Scylus stops to the right of a large, gunmetal door.

Leonidas doesn't even have to be told, to know where it leads.

Scylus waves his hand across the door, bringing up a small holo-keyboard composed entirely of blue light. Setting a sequence of button inputs into the fire-blue hologram, heavy locks on the doors suddenly click and unlatch.

Jets of steam shoot out from slots on the side of the door as it begins to move and slowly start to slide open.

PSSSSSSSSHHH!...

Entering the lab, Leonidas is greeted by the situation at hand.

All around him, scientists desperately rush trying to utilize the last remaining pockets of energy stored inside the the dying diamond of the Transmutation Matrix.

Scylus calmly walks through the lab, with both hands

behind his back, almost oblivious to the chaos and panic happening around him.

"Come, Leonidas," Scylus exclaims like one might to a pet.

And Leonidas follows reluctantly, grinding his teeth in the process.

All around them, hundreds of guards stand armed, shooting dirty looks at the man who had bested them all earlier—naked...

Cerix quietly watches Leonidas and Scylus from across the lab.

Approaching the center of the lab, Leonidas is awed by the two large towers looming over everything like two metal giants standing ready to come to life...

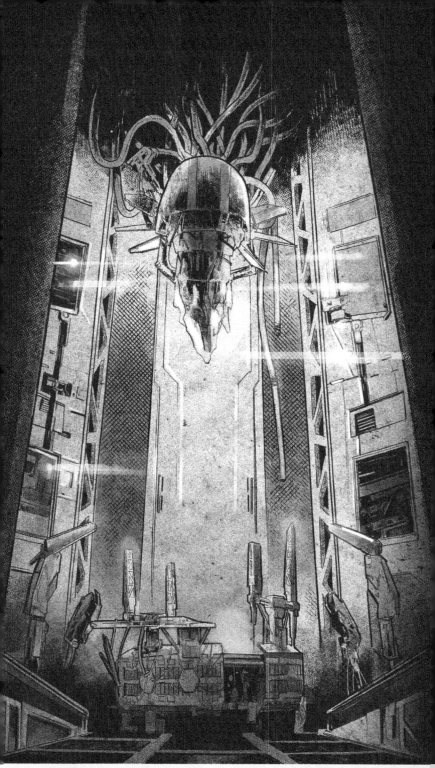

7

Multicolored light patterns pierce through the towers at various intervals, giving the subtle illusion that the two giants are thinking...

Stopping just a few feet short of the large circular platform, Leonidas looks up and sees the pale, rough diamond parabolically hanging isolated overhead.

The diamond gives off a faint, visual pulse...

Leonidas turns his head over to Scylus.

Scylus just stands there, looking up with no discernable expression across his face to allow you to try and guess what he's thinking.

The green honcho tilts his head and, looking over his shoulder, calls out to the lab in a stern, audible tone.

"How much longer now before we will be ready to proceed?!"
A voice answers back from the crowd of scientists.
"All fossil data has been analyzed and inserted!"
it says.
"DNA sequences have been solved and confirmed!"
another cries out.
"Retro activation of anatomical structures is set to initi-
ate!"
Confirms a third.
"Then let's begin," Scyles casually announces, spreading
his arms out welcomely.
Leonidas watches as the two towers suddenly begin to
hum and come to life kicking off the loud concerto of
deep mechanical groans the same as before...
The Spartan watches as the same processes that gave *him*
life suddenly begin to play out in front of him...
Standing in a mist of odd sounds and different colored
lights, Leonidas begins to feel held tight by the spectacle.
The Spartan fights to keep his cool despite the overwhelming anxiety building up inside him...
Over the large circular platform, a small electrical storm
unfurls.
It crackles and crashes, ripping the air around it in loud,
deafening tones.

KLCK-KRIK-CLASHHH!!!

Moments pass, and everything seems to be going as
planned, with no indication from anywhere that anything
is faulty.
As the storm begins closing in on itself just as it did
before, emotions in the lab run high as science closes in
trying to swipe *more* souls from fate and make a hasty

retreat home before being noticed.

The road to life is paved on a clandestine plane known only to magic and number.
A narrow stretch, rising high, on top of that which lies between both Heaven and Hell.

CLICK!—
BOOOOM!!!

Crunching down to a singularity, the electrical storm ceases shrinking and quickly reverses, bursting as it violently expands.
The entire lab is suddenly swallowed up by an enormous explosion consisting of waves of hot orange light and a sea of thick, blinding gray smoke!
The entire lab is enveloped by smog.
Leonidas tried to focus his eyes while reaching out through the haze, catching sight of Scylus for an instant trying to do the same thing.
The thick fog makes it hard for anyone to breathe.
In the lab, voices around Leonidas frantically call out to friends and coworkers.

As the smoke begins to settle, Scylus orders everyone to be quiet, and all stand unknowingly inches away from each other...
Emergency vents in the lab suddenly switch on, expelling most of the smoke and allowing things to gradually come back into focus.
As Leonidas begins to wonder about Scylus, he turns around to find the green honcho picking himself up off the floor...
As Scylus dusts himself off, he stops and stares beyond

Leonidas, as a bold set of feet gradually make their way
out of the dwindling smokescreen...

A strong pair of legs rise to reveal a man with a size and
shape similar to Leonidas's.
His smooth face differs from the Spartan King's, but his
eyes, just as intense, scan the lab from left to right as if
trying to make his mind up about the soldiers and scientists...
More and more bodies emerge from the smoke.
Each one, coming in top physical form.

"So these are the famous Spartans,"
Scylus impishly cites...
A vague sense of familiarity overtakes Leonidas,
but,
just as he is about to say something,
one Spartan in front of the rest lets out a base, guttural
roar.

"Groahhhhhrgh!!!"

The other Spartans behind him erupt in a rage,
and all at once charge forward towards the soldiers and
scientists...

The lab explodes into a frenzy as the Spartans and Scylus's men clash in a huge mash that makes it hard for the
guards to effectively discharge their weapons.
Several Etherians are caught in the mix, and Cerix runs
and hides behind some neighboring machinery.
The scene is a madhouse of curses and yelling as the
guards try hard to fight off the mob of Spartans.
Leonidas can only watch for so long before bursting into

a sprint and immediately charging forward in the direction of the mayhem.

Taking a warriors leap, Leonidas clears the heads of all those fighting and lands dead center in the heart of the melee...
Deep from within the center of the fighting, a loud and powerful voice suddenly calls out.

"Spartannnnnns!!!"

The fighting stops almost instantly, with all eyes fixed exclusively on Leonidas.
After a few tense seconds, the lead Spartan in front of the rest slowly approaches, stopping just a few feet short of him...
Staring holes into the Spartan King, mutters and murmurs rise like fog from amongst the Spartans as they all discuss the authenticity of the man standing in front of them.
From the disheveled floor of the lab, several voices talk amongst each other.
"Looks like him."
"How can it be?"
"Is this some kind of trick?"
"I don't like the looks of this..."
The Spartan in front of Leonidas suddenly walks even closer.
Face to face, the two of them square off with neither relinquishing the slightest intent of backing down...
As tension peaks, it is then suddenly brought down when the lead Spartan in front of Leonidas begins uttering,
"We fight for our king..."
Not missing a beat, Leonidas formally adds to the lead

Spartan's words.

"And we die for our country."

"Let our reasons be understood,"

the lead Spartan adds.

"And our sacrifices noted," Leonidas finishes.

And with that,

as if the words are enough to quell his suspicion, the lead Spartan gradually backs off.

Stepping back,

the lead Spartan lowers his head and falls to one knee prompting all the other Spartans in the bashed lab to follow.

As Leonidas looks around the room,

analyzing the spectacle,

he is suddenly affected by an overwhelming sense of pride in his men.

Looking down down towards the floor,

the Spartans kneeling in the lab don't see it but they hear it.

The rallying call.

The sound all Spartans make before and after every engagement.

"Harrooooh!!!..."

The call comes from their king.

In an instant,the kneeling Spartans all rise to their feet.

Raising their arms up triumphantly they all simultaneously answer the sound of their king's call.

Harrooooh!!!... Harooooh!!!...

Harrooooh!!!... Harooooh!!!...

Scylus watches from the sidelines with a cold, devilish grin as the Spartans all gather, talk, and laugh in warm, heartfelt reunion.

"And so it begins," Scylus cites quietly to himself.

"I wonder,
how many of them will give me the pleasure of watching them suffer in battle prior to death taking them again, in the name of the greatest regime the universe has ever witnessed."

Scylus sighs as he bites his lip and eye squints with ecstasy.

"I can't wait..."

8

Back on the bridge, a handful of Spartans join Leonidas and Scylus as the ship completes its last stretch of galaxies on route to Argoss...

It's been six days since the altercation in the lab, and since then The 300 have been briefed, fed, and currently hold up in the accommodations deck reserved for high ranking officials and special guests.

Each deck is specially fitted with a ward manned by crew who serve as curators of grooming and personal hygiene. The Spartans have all been shown how to bathe and given garments to wear with only slight variations existing between theirs and Leonidas's.

The Spartan King now walks with a trimmed beard, and his hair clipped and tied back to assist with his vision.

"It looks good!" a crewman candidly states, whose shape, despite being alien, is obviously female.

Alpheus, a tough, high ranking Spartan, still not used to the variety of intelligent life now known to exist, unofficially patrols the bridge, shooting distrusting glances at Scylus's crew as he walks past their stations...

With fierce, battle hardened eyes, Alpheus turns over to Scylus who stands poised across the room, looking down at a monitor screen.

"Just what sort of person is this Lord Melech? And what the hell is so special about him anyways?..."

Scylus turns to look at Alpheus and slowly walks over to him displaying the subtle contours of a smile gently carved across his face...

"He's the leader of my planet," Scylus says.

"And soon to be the leader of all planets," he continues...

"Given the budding reformation of the cosmos, it is only a matter of time before the universe is spared from itself by the compassionate rule of Argoss..."

Alpheus shoots a suspicious look at the decorated ship captain but, before Alpheus can say anything else, he is suddenly cut off by the sounds of sirens and the excited voice of a crewman calling to Scylus.

"Argoss within sight, my captain!"

"Excellent!" Scylus says.

"Prop the image up on the screen!"

Across the large central monitor at the front of the bridge, the image of a large, copper-colored planet bound by curves of blue oceans suddenly appears...

Its bright, amber-gold aura serves as the backdrop for the hundreds of warships and black watchtowers orbiting around it.

"This is Argoss," Scylus says.

Warmed by a massive makeshift sun burning bright in the distance, Argoss functions independently and uses this fact as a testament to their indomitable will and intent to rule beyond the lifespan of a solar system...

As the ship comes closer and closer, the handful of Spartans on the bridge watch with a bold sense of wonder, and awestruck skepticism.

Leonidas and them watch as details of the planet grow clearer, and clearer.

Orbiting Argoss, the Spartans all catch glimpses of the planet's large canyon peaks sitting on top of arid valleys fostering gardens of beautiful cities reaching upwards in a grand amalgamation of bright lights and strange alien metal.

Scylus looks over at Leonidas who stands firm on the bridge.

The Spartan King's appearance is even more noble standing next to an awestruck Alpheus.

Scylus points to a large populated area the central monitor on the bridge zooms in on.

"There is where we will land."

Leonidas eyeballs the city with mild suspicion.

As Cylus orders the crew to ready the ship for landing, crewmen on board react just as fast bringing up landing coordinates, initiating atmospheric re-entry protocol, and sending word out to all decks that they are bringing the ship down...

Scylus takes his seat on the captain's chair.

Looking to one side, Scylus smiles at the sight of two Spartans standing, looking around anxiously.

"Heh, you might want to hold on to something," the honcho advises while proudly gesturing for Leonidas to join him on a seat next to his own.

Leonidas declines, opting instead to stand by his men as crew on board steady ready the ship for landing.

Just then—

"Sir!

Landing mechanisms primed and remain on standby!" an officer calls out.

 "Good," Scylus says.

"Get us out of Orbit!

Follow descent course and activate atmospheric dampers and inertial restraints!

When ready... take us down... "

Tilting thirty degrees, the ship commences its descent into Argoss.

Met by the hot blanketing atmosphere, the ship is rocked by turbulence sending some of the Spartans on the accommodations deck flat on their backs as they're propelled to the floor.

"Ooomf!!!"

On the bridge, Leonidas finds the edge of a command terminal to hold on to.

Plummeting towards the ground at breakneck speed, while navigating their descent as a ninety ton fireball, lights inside the ship suddenly begin flickering sporadically.

"A standard cause from re-entry into the planet," Scylus says, sensing apprehension in some of Leonidas's men.

Grinding through the heat and steel crushing force, the ship finally breaks through the atmosphere.

Emerging intact, the ship swiftly rides the winds of the descension course, rocking casually from side to side...

"We're through!" one officer excitedly declares, and the
ship travels onward across valleys and cliffs, hugged
by the sun as it peaks from between two towering rock
formations...
jettisoning forward, the ship enters a clearing where the
edge of the city greets them from beyond a wide stretch
of rivers and fields.

"We're almost there," Scylus says with a calm anticipation, as the image on the screen reveals a beautiful, dense
metropolis of bright lights and large glistening skyscrapers.

Each building climbs higher than the next the closer it
stands towards the center where three massive gold towers rule over them from deep within the heart of the city.

Outside the southwestern edge of the city, at a bustling
import/export hub stretching thousands of miles, hundreds of different kinds of ships constantly come and go
docking to refuel, re-supply, and sell off their latest cargo
taken from some of the farthest reaches of Arogss's conquered planets...

Scylus's ship is just about there when he suddenly looks
up.

"Prep docking procedures and ready the landing struts.
We've just about arrived..."

Slowing down to normal speed, the ground around the
hub is sand-peach, bleached by the thrusters of hundreds
of thousands of ships constantly coming and going.

The ship lowers its landing struts, getting ready to dock
down on an open spot at the import/export hub.

Hovering around a sectioned drop zone, the ship gradually lowers itself, activating stabilizers to keep from leaning
off balance...

Dust is kicked up,

and a light *JERK* is felt on the bridge as the ship touches down onto the drop zone.

Leonidas and his men look at Scylus, who looks back at them all with a sneering, bold-faced grin.

"We've arrived."

A group of employees from the hub come out to greet the ship as the large cargo ramp on the back of it slowly starts to come down...

On the bridge, Scylus gets up from the captains' chair— taking a stretch before shooting a sharp glance over at Leonidas;

"Come..."

Employees from the hub hustle up the ramp, looking to secure ship personnel and unload any cargo.

Scylus and Leonidas walk down the ramp together, with Scylus talking incessantly to Leonidas too lost in thought to notice.

As Leonidas looks to his right, he is greeted by the vast alien landscape.

A sun-glaring network of blue rivers curve through rich, copper-colored fields laden with rich patches of pinks and greens generously begot by the resident flora.

Leonidas sighs deeply as he looks out, uttering quietly to himself.

"...Two years."

Coming off the ramp, Leonidas and Scylus wait for the rest of the crew to gradually make their way down...

Standing at the edge of the ramp, Leonidas waits as he watches for his men amidst all the disembarking members of Scylus's crew, in the cool arid breeze.

As the Spartans finally come down, the entire display is an awesome array of muscle and form.

Leading the way down the large cargo ramp, the Spartans

are followed next by the awkwardly, somewhat less phys-
ically impressive members of Scylus's crew.

Leonidas smirks at the droll contrast.

Alpheus leads the pack, flashing an arrogant grin and
sharp eyes that openly invite trouble and dare it to strike.

Nudging Leonidas on the shoulder with his fist as he
reaches the edge of the ramp, Alpheus and him share a
brief moment of comradery.

Reveling in their brisk moment of brotherhood,
Alpheus's eyes suddenly shift, and face boldens, swiftly
shooting a sharp glace over Leonidas's shoulders.

Standing quietly to one side, behind the two Spartans,
Scylus stands delightfully meeting Alpheus's gaze.

The honcho's hands rest pressed together at his chest,
with fingertips gracing the base of his chin.

Scylus's eyes project an impish delight, and his mouth
curves widely with a murderous satisfaction.

The honcho takes in a deep breath, sighing contently.

"Come, Spartans," he says.

"Beyond the hub stands the entrance to a building that
serves as a mandated checkpoint all must go through
before entering the city."

Marching through the chaos of the import/export hub,
Leonidas turns and looks back to get one last look at the
ship.

As Leonidas turns, he sees the Etherians who were previously on board, being led down the ramp in chains by
employees from the hub.

Their little blue faces look down in shame as their small,
shackled legs struggle awkwardly down the ramp.

Cerix leads the trek woefully,
his eyes low with humiliation...

9

Sometime later...

A recommendation from Scylus grants permission for Leonidas and his men to enter the city.

Outside the checkpoint, on the other side of the building, Leonidas and his men inadvertently walk right into the heart of a large, bustling marketplace...

All around them, dozens of little tents and makeshift shops have set up looking to trade in the latest interplanetary goods coming off of the ships that came through the import/export hub.

The Spartans pause for a moment to take in their surroundings.

Everywhere they look, *thousands* of different faces and

body types from around the cosmos mingle with each
other in the daily hustle and bustle of everyday life on
Argoss.
A menagerie of skin tones, appendages, eyes and fashion
sense come together in an eye widening display Leonidas
has never seen...
Scylus suddenly breaks out from in front of the Spartans.
"Follow me..."

Leading them through a network of endless slums, the
Spartans all get a firsthand look at the fringe bowels of
Argoss.

All around them, the festering patchwork of bright-
ly fleshed poor lay frail in the streets among shells of
wrecked vehicles and dilapidated buildings.
Residents look up at the Spartans as they march, from
under brown, faded blankets.
Leonidas looks up at one of the large gold towers as it
looks down on all from its height deep within the center
of the city...
Entering a block where the residents there are not so sick-
ly and gaunt, Scylus is bombarded by praises from the
emaciated locals that total it.
Yells fat with accolades are tossed across the street at the
olive-toned honcho as locals stop to bow or just to salute
him.
Leonidas studies these exchanges, noticing something
odd about all those stopping to honor Scylus.
They're afraid of him.
While the smile Scylus gives the crowd reflects a mild
charitable disposition, the Spartan King can see the rope
burns and lash scars on the chests and wrists accompany-
ing the eyes and grins attempting to seem delighted of the

locals giving their support to the passing ship captain.
Leonidas thinks back to the Etherians in chains...

After a long arduous walk, the Spartans cross Arogoss's
outer ring of poverty, and find themselves marching
through a grand avenue lined with beautiful buildings
rising as far as the eye can see.
Each building, painstakingly built with splendor in mind,
shines as bright as polished steel, with parts that look like
they've been painted on with melted pearls...
The scenery comes together in a lavish display of wealth
and power—balanced perfectly with the soft greenery
strategically placed throughout for added effect.
The Spartans can't help but marvel at the city, stopping
to look up at the glamorous buildings and lay gaze at the
plants' strange alien geometry.
Marching down a long, shimmering boulevard, Leonidas
can't help but notice how empty the streets are here com-
pared to the slums.
The Spartans never once run into more than a handful of
people every couple of blocks, and Leonidas finds the
streets in this part of the city eerily quiet.
The silence is unsettling...
Even on the off chance that they would run into someone,
people would just stop and stare, quietly waiting for Leonidas and his men to pass before resuming conversation
with whomever they were with...
The locals residing in this zone are all impeccably
dressed, reflecting the higher status implied by the nature
of their surroundings...
After more than two hours of marching, an irritated Alpheus suddenly decides to speak up.
"Just where the hell are you taking us?!!"

"Hmf..."

Scylus turns to look at the disgruntled Spartan.

With malevolent eyes and grin firmly affixed on Alpheus, the green honcho slowly raises his hand and extends his index finger, pointing out at something apparently lying dead ahead.

"There..."

Standing less than twenty meters away, taking up a vast clearing at the center of the city, the three gold towers come together as the three gold spires of a great, massive gold palace...

Large and imposing, the palace belittles any other building in the immediate vicinity.

"Come, Spartans," Scylus says.

"Your destiny awaits."

Standing outside the palace, the Spartans gather inside of a large courtyard teaming with dozens of tall, armed, ape-like beings serving as guards for the grounds.

Blue-skinned, white-furred, and lightly armored, the strange alien primates flare their teeth and strange blades at the large army of Spartans.

Standing only a few feet from the massive doors of the palace, Scylus raises his arms to address The 300...

"I alone and your king will be the ones entering the palace!

The rest of you will stay here...

If you have any complaints, you may take them up with any one of *them* standing among you," the green honcho says, gesturing towards the guards.

...?!

AHAHAHAHAHAHAHAH!

A hearty mix of laughter and protest breaks out from the majority of Leonidas's men.

"We'll never leave our king!"

"My, aren't we confident!"

"Is this some kind of joke?!"

"Can't guarantee your men will still be alive by the time you come back! Ha-ha!"

The courtyard is alive with bouts of sarcasm and mockery as Leonidas suddenly steps in to calm the boisterous ribbing.

"Spartannnsss!!"

......

With that, The 300 quiet their rambunctious rants, and Alpheus confidently walks over to Leonidas...

"You just say the word... and we'll die bringing this whole bloody city down to its knees..."

Leonidas sighs, separating from Alpheus, touched by the sentiment.

"There will be no need for that—yet," he replies.

"Wait here and stand by for my orders.

This shouldn't take long..."

Leonidas joins Scylus to enter the palace, while the Spartans wait everready for the worst should it happen.

The Palace's two massive gold doors slowly open, and Leonidas and Scylus go in leaving the Spartans anxiously waiting outside in the center of the courtyard...

Minutes beyond the entrance to the palace, Leonidas is surprised to notice the lack of decoration covering the walls inside.

Aside from the walls being made from the same gold that lines the outside walls, the halls inside the palace are all completely identical: bare, stripped of any discernible differences that could stimulate the senses.

The halls themselves are really more like tunnels,

Leonidas realizes.

Each hall would split up into four separate tunnels that would, in turn, then split up into four more!

"Some of these halls loop around," Scylus says, "So those who don't know their way around could be lost forever trying to navigate them.

This is a strategic aesthetic of course, designed to inhibit intruders from immediately locating the central chamber..."

After long, mind numbing swirls, and twists and turns, Leonidas and Scylus walk down a long hall whose end consists of two black chrome doors secured heavily by a squadron of twelve more of those blue-toned ape-like guards same as outside.

As Scylus and Leonidas approach, Leonidas can see that the doors are both intricately carved showcasing images of fierce serpent-like creatures with razor sharp teeth.

The twelve guards stand aside as soon as they see Scylus approaching.

As Scylus goes to open the door, he suddenly stops to collect himself before turning around to look at Leonidas...

Scylus's voice is sharp and very straightforward as he focuses solemnly on the Spartan King.

"Are you ready?" he says.

"Beyond these doors waits the future head of the entire universe.

The undisputed grandmaster of Argoss, without which we would have never gotten the machine commissioned that brought you and *your* men back from the dead.

When we finally do go in there and you see him for yourself, do yourself a favor... show some respect...

He has more power than he lets on..."

Scylus pushes the doors open and he and Leonidas proceed, taking their first steps into seeing Lord Melech.

Walking across a small entrance hall, Leonidas and Scylus emerge inside a massive circular chamber.

Leonidas's jaw parts involuntarily at the raw decadence of the room.

Dipped in gold.

Save for the granite stone arches wrapping around the circumference of its shape, the chamber warns those uninvited by way of another one of those serpent-like creatures painted massively spiraling all the way down across the floor.

Leonidas notices arches leading outside the room, hinting to more than one way of entering the chamber...

"Come, Leonidas!" Scylus says, leading the way across the floor towards an incredibly tall set of steps on the other side of the room.

Scylus stops at the center of the floor, dropping to one knee.

Raising his head, Leonidas can see the steps leading up to a solid gold throne where a marble-fleshed, lightly armor-clad figure with long, moon-silver hair sits ominously looking down from the steps at Leonidas and Scylus...

How did I not notice him before? Leonidas wonders, as the being stands up and addresses the two.

"Welcome!..."

The being makes his way down the long opulent steps, his long forest-green cape flowing gracefully over his dark rhino-steel armor...

Moving with a sudden enthusiasm he not once tries to conceal, the long haired individual joyfully crosses one half of the room, joining Leonidas and Scylus.

"It's good to see you again, Captain Scylus," the being says in a warm, amiable tone.

"You may rise."

Leonidas studies the shape of the person standing in front of him now casually chatting away with Scylus.

Broad,

hugged by strange porcelain flesh, the being's pigment is split by a black tone that retracts down his jawline and neck from the ends of his pointed ears.

Leonidas watches Scylus look up loyally at the being looking back down at him artfully with sharp eyes and a witty grin.

This has to be the one Scylus was talking about.

The Spartan King's eyes awaken as the being then turns his head and meets them with cunning focus.

"Is this him?" the being kindly asks, never breaking his gaze, awaiting word from Scylus.

"Yes, my lord."

It is him...

Melech walks over with a laxed sneer and benign eyes, placing both hands on top of the Spartan king's shoulders, looking him over.

"Interesting..."

Looking up at the one towering over him now looking down at him curiously, Leonidas is fixed on the seven foot host's imposing frame.

"I've never seen a dead person who isn't a dead person anymore," Melech says.

"I have so many questions to ask... as I'm sure you do as well..."

The upper part of Melech's face is marked by five red rings and a sixth inside the biggest, a stark galaxy-yellow. His eyes are a noontime sapphire-blue that glint as he squints in Leonidas's gaze, appraising him carefully.

"...Right," the Spartan king awkwardly states, sneering guardedly, stubbornly struggling within to acknowledge

Melech's established authority.

Melech sees this and smiles as his brow frowns fancifully, amused.

"Hmf...

You really are quite the showcase, I must say, Leonidas. Here you stand,

a living promise to one day abolish the damnable backlash of mortality.

You're a pioneer in your own right even if you yourself don't realize it."

He thinks I'm inept.

A tense left eye and a stretched half smirk preceds a strengthened posture and words from the Spartan king.

"What I *realize* is that you like to visualize a world without death in it.

Nonetheless it means nothing to me if mine isn't alive with *my* loved ones...*"*

An awkward "Hmf" and a stiff silence, and Melech's eye's lax as his grin widens, stepping backwards towards Scylus.

Leonidas locks stares with the dual toned host who doesn't waiver for a second.

"Rest assured," Melech declares, halting his stride, raising his arms up welcomely, in front of the olive-toned honcho.

"I was well informed of your situation days before you arrived.

Scylus is excited to see what you're capable of... and so am I..."

Melech's eyes are warm and confident.

His grin wide and secure.

And with the rip of a lofty snicker, Melech turns his back to Leonidas and Scylus, making his way back across the chamber and up the steps to sit on his massive gold throne...

Halfway up the steps, Melech listens as Leonidas vouches for Sparta from across the chamber.

"We Spartans, have always strived at being the world's greatest warriors by way of the intensity of our training. Our skills are second to none and as it stands, we have an agreement with you that leans on you bringing the rest of our people back from the dead.

Now...

I don't know where you plan on sending us...

but you can be sure that by the time we return,

any resistance will have been rendered nonexistent there, and you will have gained another state for the *Argoss empire.*

How does Lord Melech feel about *that?*..."

"Ha-ha!"

Melech chuckles hard with charm and disdain, entertained by Leonidas's way with words as he freely plants himself back onto his throne.

"It feels very good indeed!"

Melech affirms, leering cheerfully down at the Spartan, legs spread, shoulders leaning.

"But first I'd like to see a demonstration of what you can do..."

Leonidas's brow furrows, and his eyes sharpen.

frowning and smiling at the same time, the Spartan king eagerly leans forward slowly, with his entire being geared towards Melech.

"What did you have in mind?..."

10

"Yeaahhhhhh!!!!"
"Wooo-hooo!!!"
"Alrightttt!!"
"Yeah!"

Later that day, outside the massive walls of a densely
packed colosseum located in the northern part of the city,
the loud cheers from an immense crowd can be heard
echoing throughout the streets...
Inside the large oval stadium, thousands have already
gathered to witness the battles and gladiatorial events just
announced hours ago...
Armor and weapons clash in a maelstrom of clangs as

competitors drop to the ground in shame while others walk away from the scene, following cheers and gleaming with absolute victory.

Lord Melech has offered attendees today time away from their bland normal brand of everyday life for a free day chock full of fun and excitement...

Melech sits in a Large booth closest to the stadium ground, where he can get a first rate view of all of the fighting...

Scylus sits next to him along with a handful of dignitaries that all make up the rest of Lord Melech's party.

Inside the walls of the massive stadium, Leonidas and three of his men get ready inside one of the large prep chambers prepared for rumbling combatants.

Alpheus is among those with him...

"Soo what exactly are we doing here again?" the surly Spartan remarks.

"Melech wants to see a demonstration of what we can do. So he's arranged for us to go up against four of his best fighters." Leonidas replies.

"Yeah, I understand *that*.

But that doesn't explain why we have to go out wearing this *ridiculous* armor!" the cross Spartan says in regards to the large, bizarre, alien armor issued to him and the other three Spartans inside the prep chamber.

Its peach, coral shade stained with patches of old dirt give the chest piece an almost organic quality depraved only by the sight of six spikes sticking out like pikes from each side by the ribs.

The armor around the legs, instead, is a dry mud shade that fits snug around the waist and gleams with an almost unseen set of seven different colors discretely from between articulations along the hips, knees, and feet.

The wrist guards are tight, burgundy, and lined with fur,

while the helmet bears a striking resemblance to those worn in Sparta.

Alpheus sneers at the dare in similarity diversified more only by the two spikes at the top of the lid, whose tips stick out wielding a strange assortment of beige feathers,..

Leonidas rips the belts binding the two parts of the chest piece to him.

"We don't!"

"Huh?!"

Alpheus watches Leonidas toss the burdensome chest piece and wrist guards off to one side and turn towards him sporting only a helmet and leg armor around his entire lower half.

"Going out in that," Leonidas says, gesturing down at the thrown chest piece, "I can only see the ones on the other side of my rage feeling thankful for it."

"Heh!"

The whole thing stirs a smirk across Alpheus's face and he gladly starts to rid himself of the cumbersome chest piece as well.

Alpheus rips the straps attaching the wrist guards to his forearms and tosses them with disregard off to one side.

"And what about these two?" Alpheus says, aiming his thumb at the other two Spartans who have begun to quietly follow suit, removing their wrist guards and armor...

"Dienkes and Eurytus are a welcomed addition to any squadron," Leonidas asserts.

"Dienkes's bravery is second to none, and Eurytus's severed eye is a testament to his willingness to sacrifice life and limb for king and country.

A Spartan king would be selfish to be willing to stand and ask for more than that."

Dienkes and Eurytus say nothing...

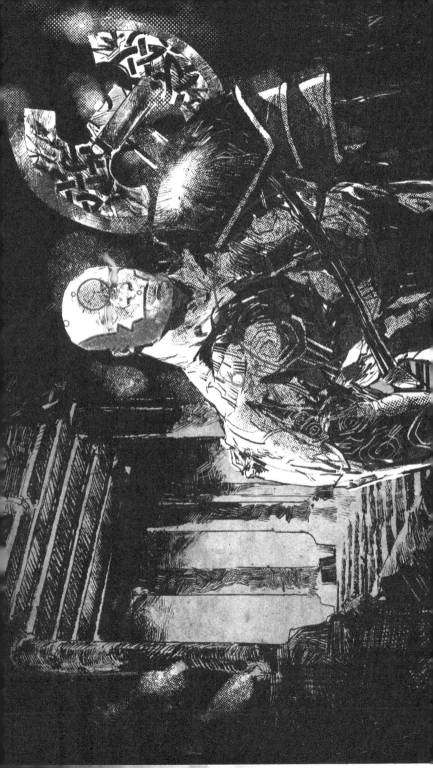

Just as the Spartans are finishing up inside the prep chamber, Leonidas and his men are suddenly given a warm greeting by a large rock-bodied alien carrying a large dual ax over his shoulders.

"Hey there!" the sediment being puts forward in a friendly baritone voice.

"I'm Brachias.

You guys new?.."

Brachias stands 6'6", with a large frame gripped by brown leather belts around his chest, that hold a large gardbrace down over one of his massive stone shoulders...

"I'm up next!

You guys be careful out there when it's your turn.

A lot of tough competition this time around."

Brachias's kind, bayou-green eyes betray his large jagged exterior. And his flash-white rock flesh stretching up the top portion of his face, and nine rings singed throughout it, a hot hateful red, is anything but settling.

Leonidas smiles at the curious contrast, replying to the stone warrior in kind.

"Tbh I'd like to see how our skills measure up against theirs...

Try not to get killed out there."

"Heh, I heard *that*," Brachias replies, hanging the large ax over his back and adjusting one of the straps lying under the gardbrace over his shoulder.

Smiling one more time at the four, the large stone warrior departs, making his way outside towards the arena...

The Spartans have all finished getting ready when Leonidas announces "Let's go,"

and all head from the prep chamber out to the warriors' stable...

The warriors' stable:
a large, hot, rancid hall housing the warriors coming from battle or waiting to compete.
The air is a warm, pungent mesh of sweat and blood, drafted solely by the massive arched opening on the far end where competitors pass through.
The pale breeze from the opening offers a short relief to all exposed to the body odor of those of countless different species...
Walking through the patches of what Leonidas assumes to be hay scattered across the solid, clay-red stone floor, the Spartans are greeted by the painful cries of the defeated...

"Arghhh!!!"

Whether being treated for their wounds or beaten for their loss. The sound is encompassing and impossible to ignore.
From the corner of his eye, Leonidas spots a competitor chained to the floor, being mercilessly whipped and taunted by a short, stout, pig-nosed guard on one side of the stable.
The guard barks, "This is how we reward those for cowardice!"

CRACK!!!

The sound of the lash reverberates palpably around the room.
Leonidas looks at the guard but holds back, lest his sympathy go ahead and cloud his better judgment.
After all,
cowardice *must* be punished.
That is Spartan law.

And Spartan law is absolute no matter where it manifests.

"Hey!!! You four!!!"

"?!.."

Leonidas turns his head to the sound of a gargled, gruff voice commanding the attention of he and the other three Spartans.

"You guys are up next!

Weapons registration is that way!"

The voice comes from a large, portly faced guard with short, yellow tusks, and an elephant's snout.

The guard churlishly gestures towards a corner on the other side of the stable, where an Etherian stands waiting outside of a small, weapons storeroom...

Walking towards the storeroom, Leonidas recognizes the Etherian standing outside of it from the ship.

It's Cerix!

Outside of his white lab coat, wearing instead an old, brown, hooded robe over the majority of his person, the Etherian flinches slightly as the four Spartans approach. Sensing his anxiety, Leonidas's eyes relax, smiling sharply with empathy at the blue being who barely goes up to his knee.

"Greetings," goes the Spartan king.

"You're one of the ones from the ship, aren't you?..."

"U-Uh,

w-well,

Yes.

Y-Yes!" the Etherian replies.

"I-I'm Cerix.

You are all from the ship as well.

How has Argoss been treating you?.."

Leonidas studies the Etherian's face, and sees an overwhelming sadness hiding behind Cerix's pathetic attempt at smiling.

"It's hard to say," rebuttals the Spartan king.

"Ever since we've arrived it's been one thing after the next."

"That makes sense," Cerix says.

"There is no rest for its prisoners on Argoss..."

Prisoners?...

The word burns a hole in Leonidas's mind.

Prisoners...

"So I guess this is it then," Cerix says, looking down as little tears begin forming, closing his eyes tightly, fighting their flow.

"(Sniff)... What a joke."

"Huh?"

Leonidas pivots his head, looking down dumbfounded at the sobbing Etherian.

"Blessed with the power to preserve life, only to turn around and be forced to destroy it."

"What are you talking about?" resounds Leonidas.

"It wasn't always like this, you know.

Back on our home world we Etherians lived a harmonious existence with the forces of the cosmos...

My people revered life, and dedicated ours to tending to all of the various forms of it that inhabited our planet.

For our efforts,

the universe rewarded us with a vast understanding of the inner workings of things, and it wasn't long before our society flourished in a blossoming utopia...

For a while, everything was *fine*.

My people thrived in isolation, with no general contact with the outside world...

Then the ships came...

We all watched as, one day, a large fleet of ships slowly descended from the clouds and touched down on our planet...

At first we were overjoyed.

We had never encountered other intelligent life and so we were all eager to meet these exciting new strangers.

Ignorance,

as we would learn,

is not limited only to the intellectually inept...

11

"A large portion of us gathered outside the ships, and we watched as one of the doors of one gradually hissed as it slid open.

Someone came out of it next, smiling, with his arms spread out to all us.

It was Scylus...

Scylus was intrigued by the complexity of our cities, and it eventually came to where he convinced our leaders to arrange for him to take a tour through one of them.

We were so naive...

In our eagerness to please, we graciously obliged, and couldn't wait to show our new friends all the beautiful things the universe had blessed us with...

We ignorantly took Scylus through Lanoren, our most precious city, and watched as his face would light up with ever growing fascination...

After the tour, Scylus then asked to be taken back to his ship, where he said he had a great proposal there waiting for us.

We took him back to his ship, from which outside of it he then unveiled his 'great proposal' to us.

Build weapons for Argoss, was his appeal.

And in exchange, he claimed he could make my people rich beyond all imagining.

My people hold a strong reverence towards life, and the taking of any feels abhorrent to us.

So we declined...

We would not apply our minds to build weapons.

Our leaders conveyed to Scylus that Etherians do not believe in war.

And to build weapons of any kind seemed redundant to us, much less building them for others.

That's all Scylus needed to hear...

The ships eventually left.

But within a week came back, and brought death and destruction down on our planet.

I can still hear the screams of all those who ran for their lives as the ships fired upon them on that horrible day..."

Standing attentively keen with his three men inside the warriors' stable, Leonidas listens to the dismal words of the perturbed Etherian.

"And so now we're here.

Forced to use our minds to build weapons, and bring life to every twisted machination Lord Melech conceives.

Make no mistake, Spartan," Cerix utters, trembling.

"Neither Scylus nor Lord Melech intend to do anything

for you.

Lord Melech is a liar and Scylus is no different!"

The four Spartans watch as Cerix bends forward, holding his stomach as his teeth gnarl and eyes clinch with tears.

"Scylus had never intended to do what he said!

This existence is exactly what he had in store for us from the very first moment he ever stepped foot on my planet! And now it's too late.

My people are fewer, and our minds and bodies weak from the never ending work and lack of sleep coupled with the sloppy nutrition from the rank rations given to us."

Cerix wipes the tears from his eyes before lifting his robe, revealing the chains fastened securely around the lengths of his ankles.

"There is no more hope left in me these days.

My advice to you, is to get as far away from here as you can...

I asked the universe for a second chance at life, once...

I never got an answer."

Cerix looks up, his eyes glazed as they gaze softly at Leonidas.

"But you...

You seem to have garnered its favor.

Do not waste this opportunity.

The universe doesn't give many second chances at life.

It must have plans for you.

Perhaps it is—"

"Hey! what's the hold up?!!"

"..?!"

The gargled, gruff bellows from the large, elephant-nosed guard infiltrate the space occupied by the four Spartans and Cerix.

Cerix grabs his robe by his chest, stepping forward one

step, petitioning Leonidas...

"Run...

Do it!

Before you and your men are forced to work in some labor camp or made to join the army and die looking up at the black sky of some dark, forsaken planet..."

"Spartans! You're up!" the guard says.

"Remember what I said," Cerix implores.

Cerix quickly turns and vanishes into the storeroom, and comes out dragging a large circular shield with another one of those snake-like creatures emblazoned in red at the center...

Cerix quickly goes in and out, dragging more and more weapons until he has four swords and four shields laid out in front of the Spartans.

"Here, take these!" Cerix says, gesturing towards the lot.

Leonidas reaches down...

Picking up one of the swords, Leonidas holds it up close towards his face to inspect it.

"We analyzed parts of the book you are mentioned in," Cerix says.

"So we know that you all are used to fighting with weapons like these.

However...

These weapons were forged using Etherian techniques, and so their metals can withstand the most prominent beam weapons...

Weapons like these are still used today, mind you— but they are by no means the norm...

As such, they are developed to compete in the changing times.

The four Spartans scrutinize the tools expected to use in battle, as Cerix enlightens them with a concise utterance highlighting the nature of their make.

"Your blades are pretty straight forward—literally; linear, with a hilt and blade ratio that provides perfect weight distribution to the user with each thrust..."

Leonidas tightly grips the blade handle, feeling a surge throughout his body that is all too familiar.

The Spartan king can hardly contain himself.

"Let's go..."

Sliding one of the shields onto his forearm, Leonidas disembowels the air with his stare, initiating the march from the small weapons storeroom towards the outside arena.

"Good luck," Cerix peeps, fidgeting timidly as the shadows from the other three Spartans flow over him as they pass...

Stepping out into the arena, the Spartans are greeted by the cheers and howls of a rambunctious crowd consisting of a million different people from a million different planets...

Looking out pensively at the crowd, Leonidas and his men slowly make their way towards the center of the arena...

A beige-skinned alien draped in a strange black outfit akin to a suit, wearing different colored visors over both sets of eyes, prominently stands at the center of one of the lower stands lying closest to the floor that holds the fighting.

The dapper alien announces,

"Laddiieeeeeees annnnnnnnnddd gentlemennnnn!!!"

The crowd's excitement grows even louder.

"Please welcome!!!

Fighting for the first time in Argoss's battle arena!!!"

Leonidas looks up and sneers at the announcer.

"The mighty...!!!

The powerful...!!!

The fearless...!!!
Spartannns...!!!"

The stadium explodes as cheers from the crowd rock the entire stadium at its foundation.

Looking up at the crowd, unimpressed, Alpheus narrows his eyes, frowning and smiling at the same time citing to Leonidas.

"Pshhh, these creatures don't even know who we *are...*"

"That's okay, Alpheus, Leonidas says.

By the time we're all finished here they will never forget us..."

"Annnd nowww...!!!
Welcoming them back to the battle arena!!!
Argoss is privileged, honored,
and proud to announce!!!
The insidious!!!
Spectacular!!!
Undisputed champions and bloodthirsty fiendddsss!!!"

The crowd listens as the beige announcer's voice becomes growled and guttural.

"The wretched Ceryls!!!..."

The crowd follows suit, and their cheers get low as they welcome the Ceryls with committed, bass-fueled celebration.

"Rooooh!" "Grrrrrrrr!" "Yehhhhhhhh!" "Ha-ha!..."

Leonidas and Brachias look towards the other side of the arena where, at the other end of it, lurks another gaping arch leading into another warriors' stable...

Emerging from the depths of it, a band of six warriors gradually make their way out...

The crowd cheers as the six make their way into their sights flashing teeth as sharp and foul as the vile looks on their faces...

SPARTANS IN SPACE 01

Teal-fleshed, with psycho-orange eyes, the Ceryls' dress paints them every bit as much as a bunch of wild dessert marauders.

Two of the Ceryls stand high and hide behind cloaks with their hoods up, while all six carry metal staffs that crackle and hiss with momentary fits from the ends of them, beaming with raw red energy.

Alpheus is the first to irk and comment on their numbers.

"I thought this was supposed to be a four on four match?!"

Never taking his eyes off the Ceryls,

Leonidas replies, gnashing his teeth with frenzied excitement.

"Heh... It would seem, Lord Melech has other plans..."

Sitting in the large booth overseeing the fighters, Scylus leans over towards Lord Melech,

"I thought this was supposed to be a four on four match, my lord?..."

Reclining, looking down at Leonidas from the largest chair in the booth, Lord Melech narrows his eyes, raises an eyebrow, laughs to himself and casually replies,

"Yes...

But I thought this'd be more interesting..."

Back at the center of the arena, Leonidas steps forward, addressing the Ceryls.

"I suppose you six think you have some sort of advantage coming here with more men.

Hrmf!...

In that case you're about a hundred short!!!"

Breaking off into formation, the Ceryls move in.

With staffs crackling in sync with their monstrous screams, the team of six dash madly at the four Spartans.

In the marred mash of jeers and cheers from the crowd, four Ceryls spread across the arena as two others leap firing energy blasts ahead of the four from the ends of their staffs.

"Spartans, attack!" Leonidas yells as he rushes forward, barely evading an energy blast landing only inches away from Alpheus.

Alpheus looks down at the smoking, scorched, stadium floor.

"They're using projectiles!" Alpheus roars.

"They're cowards!" Leonidas rebuttals.

"Spartans, get up close!" Leonidas orders, halting, gathering his troops.

"We're going to show these six what *real* fighting looks like."

Alpheus grips his shield and follows up behind his king, as the four Spartans valiantly charge forward against the Ceryls.

Leonidas is just ten feet away from one of them when the Ceryl suddenly decides to jump, firing a bolt from his staff that prompts Leonidas to leap up and challenge it.

The Spartan's shield intercepts the shot in mid-air, scattering the blast.

Leonidas then grabs the Ceryl's ankle, spins, and sends him spiraling back down onto one of his teal teammates.

CRAASSHHH!!!

The result is a crowd-wrenching collision.

Dust kicks up, and two of the Ceryls are down but not out when Alpheus arrives.

One of the other Ceryls goes after the Surly Spartan.

Swinging his staff, Alpheus greets one side of it with the edge of his sword.

CLASHHH!!!...

The contact sends sparks of red light trailing through the air as Dienkes and Eurytus arrive just in time to throw down in the scrum...

Dienkes looks down, raising his sword at one of the downed Ceryls.

The Ceryl manages to kick at Dienkes's shin and swing up with his staff, making contact with Dienkes on the side of his helmet.

SMAAASH!!!

The Spartan is momentarily stunned.

Dienkes follows up with a yell and a swing down with his sword as the Ceryl twists to evade and swiftly hustles back up.

Eurytus struggles with another Ceryl just a few feet away. Both Eurytus and the Ceryl are swinging, and clashing, and kicking, and shouting, blocking, and dodging while trying to bait the other one with tricks and gain the upper hand.

"These bastards are tougher than they look!" Eurytus calls out.

"They're *nothing!*" Leonidas responds, bashing a Ceryl over the head with one end of his shield.

The crowd responds with discernable *oooooooohs!* following the audible collision.

Leondias grabs the Ceryl and tosses him at the one Eurytus is fighting.

The two Ceryls fall, and Eurytus finishes them both with a forward down thrust, courtesy of the razor front edge of his sword.

SLASH!!!...

"Now the bout is set four against four, with the Spartans advancing!" the beige alien announces.

Melech looks over at Scylus sitting next to him inside the booth,

"My, it seems like what was written in that quaint little book of yours wasn't all talk after all..."

"Hmff!..."

Scylus leans back in his chair and smiles...

12

Standing four against four, Leonidas raises his shield
while holding out his sword, stepping forward in defiance
against the enemy Ceryls...

One of the Ceryls walks directly into his gaze, wearing
a mischievous grin as if oblivious to what had just happened to his two teammates only moments ago...

"Heh,,, You can't win," Leonidas says.

"Why don't you give up now and save me the trouble of
defeating you.

That way, I won't have to feel so bad later about crushing
somebody so weak, ha-ha!..."

The remark wipes the smirk off the Ceryl's face, sending
him into a rage, emitting a high-pitched guttural sound

that resonates deep from within the center of the stadium. "IIIIIIIIIIIIIIIIIIAAAARRRRRRRGGGHHHHHHHHH!!!"
Joined by the other three, the two Ceryls with cloaks quickly removed them revealing huge pairs of bug-like wings that buzz as they flap quickly, instantly sending the two skyward.

The two Ceryls commence to rain down waves of energy blasts on top of the Spartans below.

Leonidas and his men have nowhere to run.

Crouching behind their shields, Alpheus fits with rage. "Argh! Those bastards!"

Leonidas hears his men's plight amongst the rattling of their shields, and all four are battered and bashed on all sides as they shift around to defend themselves against the relentless assault.

Leonidas peeks from behind his shield to look up, instant- ly greeted by the smash of it with a Ceryl's staff in an instant almost too quick for the Spartan king to react. Leonidas ducks behind his shield again, and looks right, only to spot something dash by him in a haze of teal.

SMASH SMASH SMASH SMASH SMASH SMASH !!!

The Ceryls have taken to great lengths to put an end to Leonidas and the other three Spartans.

As the other two Ceryls continue to rain a bright hell from above, the Ceryls below dash madly, attacking each Spartan, alternating wildy trying to draw his shield's face away from the blasts long enough to be caught by them.

SMASHSMASHSMASH!!!

Leonidas is in a tight spot and he knows it—

SMASH!

If the searing blasts barraging repeatedly don't put an end to him, then the blunt force brought on by the strength of the Ceryls' staffs will.

Splitting his attention between the blasts and attacks from

the Ceryls' staffs make it hard for Leonidas to think.
Come one, come on, come on, come on!
As one of the blasts nearly misses, Leonidas can see the
energy disperse in a red burst and burn a Ceryl on the
hand as he dashes past, catching some of the red scattering off the edge of the shield.

"Yiaaaohr!"

That's it!

As the searing torrent keeps pouring on the Spartans hun-
kered on the ground below, Leonidas waits for another
Ceryl to run past and take a swing at him.

As one Ceryl hastens in, raising his staff, in the interim
between when an energy blast rains down on Leonidas's
shield, the teal-fleshed alien's rage shapes to surprise as
Leonidas drops his sword and abruptly turns, quickly
lunging towards him.

The Ceryl has no time to react as the Spartan grabs him
and lands a full nelson that forces the Ceryl to face the
peril approaching in red.

His orange eyes open wide as the energy blast closes
in, and Leonidas lets go of the hold and kicks the Ceryl
towards it.

"Iarrrrrrrhhh!!!"

The Ceryl's face bends as his body wriggles and stiffens
before the air around him glows red and he's fully disin-
tegrated.

The move shocks the other Ceryl on the ground to stop
and move further away, blasting at the Spartans erratical-
ly in a mix of fright and hatred.

Leonidas peeks from one end of his shield and looks up,
gauging the distance between him and the two Ceryls
flying.

Void of options, Leonidas lowers his shield and takes off
running, desperately dodging bolts of red light that

relentlessly touch down and just barely miss him. Scrambling through the shimmering onslaught, Leonidas is grazed a few times on the neck and arm by the one Ceryl on the ground as he backs up and watches Leonidas inexplicably zigzagging fast past him.

The other Spartans look on, and just as Alpheus is about to move, the three are subdued by a series of blasts rising like geysers that land two feet in front of them.

Alpheus looks up as the two Ceryls look down, flying, grimacing with eyes reminding Alpheus that the two are still watching.

A flash from a blast coming from the grounded Ceryl's staff snaps Alpheus back out of it—forcing him to bring up his shield.

As Leonidas bobs and weaves, running, trying to think of something as everything blows up around him in a frenzied bombardment of hellish pulsating red, the Spartan stops and gets caught, in an instant that sees him consumed in a searing, widening dome of crimson energy.

The moment is absolute, and the flying Ceryls smile as the dome widens some more, before noticing something emerging from it, flying towards them.

The glare from the burning half sphere interferes with perception, and so all the two Ceryls see is a silhouette nearing, thin and streamline.

The moment is quick, too quick for anyone to realize, as the object closes in and clashes with the face of one of the Ceryls.

THWACK!

The impact is swift and precise, as the crowd winces at the sight of Leonidas's shield colliding with the Ceryl's face.

Ooooooh!

The Ceryl drops as the other one flying spots Leonidas

running from the searing dome that has since grown transparent and stopped widening.

The Ceryl's eyes narrow with spite as he watches Leonidas running, smoking, resolved, lively, still gripping rightly to his sword.

"Now's our chance!!!"

The three Spartans suddenly heave themselves into a sprint, in an instant viciously seized by opportunity and Alpheus's wail.

"Roahhhhhahr!!!"

The three Spartans roar fiercely as they charge, meeting the dust-launching dash carrying the grounded Ceryl now barreling towards them.

Leonidas and the flying Ceryl lock eyes as the running Spartan king now quickly hustles towards him.

The grounded Ceryl scraps his dash and transitions into a linear mash of fast flips, twists, spins and ground-treading acrobatics.

The movements are as quick as the instant it takes to close the distance, and the grounded Ceryl travels from an energized back flip into a roll that springs and launches him high above the three Spartans.

BLASTBLASTBLASTBLASTBLASTBLASTBLAST!!!

A barrage of red blots head towards Dienkes, Eurytus, and Alpheus.

The three Spartans instantly scatter, with Dienkes focusing his attention on the still airborne Ceryl with wings.

The Ceryl that fell to the ground earlier—hurt, it seems, by Leonidas's shield, suddenly wakes in a daze that sees him lay gaze to Dienkes, before sluggishly raising himself with his wings, curve wildly launching forward, and speed groggily towards him.

Dienkes spots the Ceryl flying towards him, with only

seconds to react, and jumps up, spinning, thinking only of the other Ceryl flying idly beyond.

In a move that catches the alien crowd wooed, Dienkes twirls, using the inertia to hurtle *his own* shield up at the unsuspecting Ceryl flying high over the stadium.

The moment is too quick for the groggy Ceryl to pick up on, and he zips past, forgoing his attack on Dienkes and shifting his focus on Alpheus.

The Ceryl flying up high is too caught up watching Leonidas to notice Dienkes's shield racing towards him—to the horror and excitement of the crowd.

Leonidas and the flying Ceryl share one last glance.

Running, Leonidas is almost under the Ceryl when Dienkes's shield smashes against the back of one of the Ceryl's two wings.

CRACKKKK!

The hit comes as a shock, and the Ceryl drops, falling hundreds of feet before recovering and his wings kick in to save him.

The angry Ceryl glares at Dienkes before feeling something heavy hanging from the end of his ankle.

Looking down, the flying Ceryl spots Leonidas dangling, desperately trying to hold on to the bottom of the Ceryl's leg.

The whole thing only adds to the already agitated Ceryl's fury, and so he flies back up, fast, with Leonidas still attached, climbing higher and higher and higher into the sky, spinning, with the stadium and crowd mixing into a dizzying swirl as Leonidas tries to look down at the stadium ground below.

Leonidas and the Ceryl almost disappear completely from Dienkes's sight, before he turns around and runs back to go and assist Eurytus and Alpheus.

CLASHCLASHCLASHCLASHCLASHCLASHCLASH!!!
Alpheus and the other Ceryl with wings are busy engaged in a machine gun chain of relentless weapons war.

Staff and sword clash as Alpheus and the Ceryl dash for long moments, clashing frantically in short bursts, going forward and back.

Their eyes are too focused on each other to look away, and so their peripheral vision guides them throughout their vicious melee throughout the arena.

Eurytus and the grounded Ceryl are engaged in a game of distance, with Eurytus backed against a wall as the Ceryl fires wave after wave of red bolts at him in order to maintain it.

Dienkes draws a breath, before heading off in Eurytus's direction to bring aid to his teammate—

CLASHCLASHCLASHCLASHCLASHCLASHCLASH!!!
SWIPE!
SLASH!
"Aiioooooorh!!!"

In an instant stuffed with mad action between Alpheus and the Ceryl with wings, the Spartan lands a hit that manages to sever the bottom half of the Ceryl's left arm and send it spinning—to the shock and awe of all throughout the audience.

The Spartan and Ceryl pause and stand, with the Ceryl barely reacting to the black ooze now spewing from his arm.

The Ceryl stares at the Spartan, with emotionless eyes, focusing solely on destruction despite the severity of his injury.

Both Alpheus and the Ceryl lean in and posture, slowly, watching each other, both eager to give it one more go.

The arid air barely gets a chance to blow, when it

explodes in a savage anthem of clashes and *WIFFs*
brought about by the sudden restart of the war between
the winged Ceryl and Alpheus.
They seem to be closely matched—
"Eckkk!..."
The moment is short lived.
And the whole thing is over before anyone in the audi-
ence even knows who finished it.
"Huh?"
"What happened?"
"I can't see."
"Which one of them won?"
"Are they done fighting?"
"They're standing too close together!"
Standing pressed against the other's chest, with their
necks craned over the other's shoulder, Alpheus and the
winged Ceryl alone exist in the silent hiss of post battle
climax.

Lodged between the waist and ribs is Aplheus's sword,
and the winged Ceryl its poor ill fated recipient...
The Ceryl drops to his knees, wheezing, before the rest of
life leaves him and he slowly carreens face first onto the
dust airing stadium floor...
The moment is secured, assured, and Alpheus quietly
turns and walks away with shield in tow.
There really is nothing to say.

Tackling the strength of two Spartans, across the stadium
the grounded Ceryl struggles vainly against Dienkes and
Eurytus.
The Ceryl's blasts and swipes from his staff are no match
against the two hell-bent Spartans set on keeping him at
close range.

The Ceryl's panic and desperation only rises now with the arrival of Alpheus.

In a *real* moment that almost seems sealed in the match for the anxious Ceryl, his bright orange eyes glint in tandem with a wide, madman grin.

The Ceryl snickers under his breath as he turns two thirds of his staff, emitting a high pitch metallic *CHNKK!* from it only heard slightly by Eurytus and Alpheus.

The staff starts glowing a faded white as it begins to pulsate faintly, and the Ceryl starts swinging indiscriminately at all three Spartans.

The brawling continues, with the Ceryl throwing caution to the wind, advancing senselessly with swings rather than blasting forward more hordes of red bolts to hold some distance.

Alpheus notices the pulse on the staff has started to flash quicker.

The madness continues, with the Ceryl seemingly in peril and not giving a damn.

In a hot mix of oncoming end for the teal-fleshed being, Eurytus *also* spots the staff in the Ceryl's hands pulsating much faster now.

In a moment that watches the three Spartans close in, the Ceryl suddenly springs up high, with his staff over his head, seemingly getting ready to barrel down on Eurytus and Alpheus.

Eurytus and Alpheus both draw up their shields, while Dienkes jumps up to attack, having since lost his shield after chucking it up at one of the flying Ceryls.

Dienkes reaches the Ceryl as the staff now flashes radically in the teal being's hands.

Dienkes reaches the Ceryl, and the staff quits flashing.

The Ceryl smiles at Dienkes, and he and him share a glance a half second before the four are then consumed by a huge explosion—
BOOMMMмMMM!...
The whole stadium jolts and then sways from the shock-wave emitted from where the four were just fighting.

...

Laying all the way across the stadium, separated by yards, Eurytus and Alpheus lay with their arms up, legs separated, with Alpheus slowly reaching for his forehead as he tries to take in what just happened...

"..."

Alone, but not too far from them, laying on his side across the floor, Dienkes coughs as his legs shift, giving off traces of life.
The grounded Ceryl is nowhere to be found—consumed by the blast whose boom threw the three Spartans, leaving two with bruises, cuts and scrapes.
Dienkes lays, charred on his arms, ribs, and one side of his face, his shoulder dislocated and no groans indicating it resonating from him.
Dienkes turns, searching for Eurytus and Alpheus, who have begun to sit up and look relatively okay.
Dropping a laugh at himself, Dienkes sighs as he lies back, finding humor in being the only one of the three of them suffering from actual injuries.

"Heh!
And so it is..."

Dienkes tries to stand, but goes limp, and falls back down to a seated position...

The entire stadium is filled with a low, reverberating mumble coming from the entire audience as it stands looking up at the sky, with its jaws dropped in taut anticipation.

The three Spartans look up to see what the audience is looking at.

Alpheus's eyes widen, catching first sight of what the audience's seeing.

"It's Leonidas!"

Rising high above the stands, Leonidas wrestles with the last Ceryl, fighting to get the upper hand as both viciously struggle for position hundreds of feet in the air...

Alpheus and the others can only watch helplessly as Leonidas fights from a height from which nobody can help him...

Grappling high above the stadium, Leonidas secures a body lock that stops the winged Ceryl from using his wings.

"Shit!!!" Alpheus wails, watching Leonidas and the winged Ceryl now plummeting towards the stadium floor.

"What do we do?!" Eurytus demands, turning Alpheus towards him.

Alpheus is lost for words...

Faster and faster Leonidas and the winged Ceryl race towards the stadium floor—to the dread and excitement of all those watching them.

As the speed increases, Leonidas flashes his teeth, grinning at the winged Ceryl glancing over who, only moments ago was so hell-bent on ending him.

The Ceryl fits desperately, fighting to free himself from Leonidas's grip, but it's too late!

And the two of them plummet, crashing hard as they both land solidly in the center of the stadium.

Ohhhh! the crowd recoils.

Dust is kicked up, and for a moment the stadium floor is thick with a swirling granular haze.

Alpheus gnarls as he puts his arm over his eyes, trying to navigate the mist and assist Leonidas.

"Arghh, Dammit!"

As the dust begins to settle, Leonidas's shape gradually appears, lying motionless on the floor next to the enemy Ceryl.

Alpheus rushes over, huffing, eyes glazed with worry— stopping just short of halfway by what the crowd around him is now rustling over.

"?!.."

Slowly rising from the ground, Leonidas struggles to his feet.

"My king." Alpheus rushes towards him.

Stumbling slightly, Leonidas attempts to straighten himself, looking back at the wasted Ceryl...

Mutters and murmurs among the audience quickly shift into praise and cheer as the beige alien in visors and "tux" suddenly declares victory to Leonidas and his Spartans.

"Ladieees annnd gentlemen...!!!

In a stunning upset!!!

After an unforgettable display of ability and skill!!!

Your new champions of Argoss's Battle Arena are...!!!

Theeeee...!!!

Mightyyy...!!!!

Spar-tannnns...!!!"

The audience quickly rises, vocalizing their approval: clapping and shouting, whooping and hollering as the entire stadium comes to life in massive celebration.

"Wooooooo!!!"

"Alright!!"

"Now *that's* how you do it!"

"I never doubted them for a second!"

"I can't believe how it finished!"

Leonidas limps with his first steps, looking up at the crowd as they all commence showering him with sounds of worthiness and praise...

Turning his head, searching for the best route that leads back to the warriors' stable, Leonidas spots Lord Melech standing in his booth, clapping alongside Scylus.

Leonidas and Melech make eye contact.

Leonidas just stares...

13

Lord Melech claps, looking back at Leonidas with a slim, hollow grin, and sly eyes as he and the rest of his party inside the booth honor the Spartans with a standing ovation.

Leonidas turns his head and begins to head back towards the large arch of the warriors' stable.

Alpheus runs up to his side and walks next to him.

"How are you feeling?"

"Like a warrior."

Dienkes follows closely behind, beside Eurytus.

Dienkes smiles arrogantly from victory while holding his shoulder.

The four quietly walk back to the warriors' stable amid

praises and cheers from a satisfied audience...
Leaning against the arch entrance stands Brachias with
both arms crossed in front of him.
"That was one hell of a match," he says, flashing that
benevolent grin and those warm friendly eyes, the two
betraying his hulking size and sharp, jagged exterior...
Leonidas smirks, lightly jabbing brachias on the arm with
his fist as he slowly makes his way past the arch entrance.

Entering the stable, Leonidas's thoughts begin to settle
alongside the noise from the outside as he lets out a hard
sigh and lets his muscles relax...
None of the Spartans say anything as they walk back
past the stale patches of hay strewn over carmine-colored
brick, and the ominous rows of worn, chrome chains
lying ready to receive the next of fortune's rejects.
Leonidas thinks back to the one fighter accused of cowardice and the torture he received from a guard with a
pig's nose sometime before the match.

Back in the prep chamber, Leonidas removes his helmet
before heavily planting himself onto a bench.
Spent, the Spartan king closes his eyes, taking a deep
breath, leaning back against the wall as all his muscles
relax.
"Ahhh_{hhh...}"
The other Spartans are busy removing their armor when
a small commotion is suddenly heard outside the prep
chamber.
The four Spartans get up to investigate and see what it is.

Looking out beyond the threshold of the chamber, Leonidas's eyes widen as he spots the guards with the pig's
nose, and Elephant tusks, harassing someone fastened to

the worn, chrome chains he gazed at before.
It's that fighter from earlier!
Leonidas makes out, watching as the Ceryl that hit the
ground with him prior now stands seized, trembling,
laboring to breathe.
"I bet you're really wishing you'd have won now, huh?
Ha-ha!" Mocks the guard with the pig's nose.
"Well, if he survives this," spits the guard with elephant
tusks, "I can't help but think that this whole thing will
help to serve as some kind of extra motivation, Ahahaha!"
The warriors' stable echoes with the sounds of cruel
laughter as each guard eagerly takes his turn inflicting
damage on the injured Ceryl.

THWACKKK!
"Oooof!"
PTOWW!
SLAP!
Ahahahahahahah!!!...

From out of the small, weapons storeroom on the other
side of the stable, Leonidas makes out a small rattling
coming from the edge of the entrance.
It's Cerix...
Watching from the sidelines, on the other side of the
room, the Etherian's chains clink as he shakes, terrified,
hiding inside the storeroom...
Cerix looks on at the Ceryl, as his mouth contorts and
tears from his eyes cascade while he shakes his head,
squeezing the upper part of his robe.
"If there was something I could do for you I would,"
Cerix cites to himself quietly.

"Hmff!"

Leonidas flips the back of his hand at the scene as he turns around and goes back to sit down at a bench.

An act of aggression now against an authority figure would only be taken the wrong way.

Lord Melech may start doubting my commitment towards my end of our bargain.

If that should happen, I'm sure I can kiss seeing Sparta again goodbye.

And that Ceryl isn't nearly worth the trouble...

Throwing himself back down on a bench, Leonidas tries gathering his thoughts once more, when he is suddenly interrupted by the sharp yelps from a small voice seeping its way inside the prep chamber.

"?!..."

Leonidas rises to his feet once more to investigate the ruckus, and looks out to see Cerix held upside down by the pig-nosed guard on one side of the stable.

"Eh..."

Dangling helplessly by his shackles, Cerix is mocked and harassed as he's carried off from the small, weapons storeroom, all the way down towards the Ceryl.

The pig-nosed guard snorts eagerly, laughing as he relishes the Etherian's helpless position.

"Ha-ha!

So...

You like to watch, huh?..."

Torts the pig-nosed guard.

"I bet you got a real *kick* off watching us hammer away at this poor bastard, didn't you?"

"N-No.

No!—"

Cerix tries to speak up but is just as quickly interrupted.

"Now, now!...

I'll tell you what I'm going to do..."

Since you seem to like watching so much, I'm going to do you a little favor!...

I'm going to give you a front row seat to this guy's beating by swinging you around really fast and hitting him with you a few times until you both pass out, eh?! What do you say?..."

Cerix tries to plead as his body begins to swing, turning lights into blurs among barbarous laughter.

"*Ahahahahahahahahah!!!*"

"Darn him..."

Leonidas watches bitterly the cheap narrow-minded amusement of the guards, before finally deciding to step up and manifest his grievance...

Striding towards the guards, with stone-cutting eyes, the Spartan king's teeth gnarl as he nears the sounds of the laughter.

Among the haughty, boisterous laughter, Cerix's swinging suddenly stops, and he drops, looking up groggily at Leonidas pinning the pig-nosed guard against the wall by the flesh of his shoulders.

"....?!"

Leonidas looks down at the guard, with a lofty grin, as the other three Spartans come closing in around the group.

"I couldn't help but notice how generous you were being to my little blue friend over there."

Leonidas says, gesturing towards Cerix.

"Seeing as I'm in a giving mood myself, I'm going to give your partner here a first-hand look at your own beating. And then I'm going to do the same thing to him so that he can be even with you.

What do you say?..."

Pressing the guard's shoulders against the wall, Leonidas smirks as he lets on more pressure, pressuring the pig-nosed guard to wail, as all those around him now hear his bones breaking.

The stable is filled with a high-pitch, palpable scream.

Alpheus grabs the Elephant-nosed guard from behind and holds him.

Led by the piercing loud shouts of pain, Brachias appears from the front of the warriors' stable to investigate the commotion.

"?!..."

Walking in on the mix of guards and Spartans, Brachias spots Leonidas at the center of them, pressing the pig-nosed guard up against a wall.

"Help me...!!!"

Brachias's eyes sink,

and his chin raises,

tilting his head to one side, eye-balling the guard.

"How many times had others cried the same thing, only to be met with ridicule, and answered coldly by your abuse?"

The sound of the guard's screams grow louder and louder before they're replaced by jumbled up please pathetically begging Leonidas to stop.

"Please!

Please!!

Let me go!

I'm sorry!

I'm sorry...!!!"

Lifting the guard up by his throat, Leonidas draws his fist back as his left eye locks in on the pig's nose now flowing with mucus.

"I envy you," Leonidas says.

"You're about to get more rest than I've had all day."

Gnashing his teeth, drawing back with his arm as far as his body'll reach, Leonidas, about to pile down on the

guard with all that he can muster,
is interrupted by a sudden thunderous order commandeer-
ing the air around them.
"That's enough!.."

...

All eyes in the stable look behind in surprise as Lord
Melech stands there with four guards, arms crossed,
watching them.
Leonidas puts the pig-nosed guard down and turns over to
Lord Melech.
Breaking away from his four escorts, Melech smiles as he
lowers his arms, revealing his palms as he casually makes
his way over to Leonidas.
"You'll have to forgive these two," Melech says, gestur-
ing towards the two guards.
"Their reputation among the prisoners here is—smudged,
at best."
Prisoners?...
Leonidas raises an eyebrow.
Glancing over at the pig-nosed guard now sitting col-
lapsed on the floor, Melech grimaces with one eye while
smiling dismissively.
" Hmf...
This one takes his work just a little too seriously, I'm
afraid.
?..."
The shy trembling of a quiet Cerix steals Melech's atten-
tion away for a second to examine him.
Cerix looks up, grabbing his robe, jittery, visibly shaken
by the sudden acknowledgement from Argoss's ruler.
Melech rolls his eyes and tilts his head down at him.
"You may run along now, Cerix."

Cerix gathers his chains in his arms and runs off, as Melech turns and faces Leonidas with a cold casual grin.

"You know, Cerix is pretty well known around these
parts...

Among the Etherians he is one of their top engineers,
imagine that...

Congratulations on your victory, by the way!

That's what I came in here to say.

You and your men have far exceeded my expectations.

Looks like what you said to me in my palace earlier
might be true."

"yeah?..

So what now?"

Leonidas says, crossing his arms, looking up at Melech,
in front of his three men.

Alpheus lets go of the Elephant-nosed guard and watches
him run off.

"Now?

Now?!

Ha-ha!

Now you rest," Melech says.

"Brachias!

Come!"

Melech aims a commanding finger at the large stone
warrior, ordering him to come over with a simple bend at
the tip.

"Brachias will take you over to the recovery ward to have
your wounds treated.

After about an hour or two there, you and your men will
come out feeling good as new.

I guarantee it..."

14

Trudging amongst the damp, moss-covered brick lining the walls and ceiling of a dimly lit, narrow corridor underneath the stadium, Brachias leads the team of Spartans to the recovery ward for treatment.

"I admire what you all did back there, standing up to the guards the way you all did."

Cracks in the bricks overhead shed water droplets on all, and Leonidas blinks as he's *splished* on the nose by one.

"There's nothing admirable about picking on someone as weak as that guard is," Leonidas asserts.

"I just wanted him to stop swinging that little Etherian around..."

Traversing the cracked, gravel littered floor, Leonidas squints his eyes, peering beyond Brachias at the eerie blue light emitting from a large open doorway at the end of the corridor.

"..."

As the party of five reach the edge of the frosted-blue light, Leonidas approaches the open doorway, with a slight limp and a grimace in tow.

The escaping light illuminates Leonidas's face.

Gazing into the belly of the doorway, Leonidas's eyes widen at the wall-to-wall order of huge, blue, liquid orbs floating freely in a vast room, between machines shaped like wide snub cones.

"Come on!" Brachias Says, his eyes shut into crescents, gesturing with his head for Leonidas and his men to follow him in through the doorway.

Entering the room, Leonidas is greeted by the dim, almost inaudible hums from the machines operating in almost total silence...

Leonidas studies the make of the machines and orbs as he makes his way further into the room.

"Eck!"

Craning his neck, with a sharp sneer, Leonidas stops, spotting a body churning within one orb, lifeless and limp.

Wha- What is this?...

Clenching his fist, Leonidas's head begins to sway every which way, discovering more and more bodies floating freely inside orbs.

"This is the recovery ward."

"?..."

Leonidas turns and finds Brachias standing across from him, smiling.

"All injured fighters have the chance to come here after a

match if their wounds are too severe to be treated conventionally...

But, between you and me,

I think the main reason they let us come here is to get us back out into the arena faster.

A lot less hassle to treat a seasoned fighter than to re-train a new one, you know what I mean?!"

Brachias puffs his chest and smiles confidently.

"Anyways,

Melech must have taken a real liking to you.

He never visits prisoners in the stable after they're done fighting."

Prisoners?...

Leonidas's face contorts with a *huff*, teeth flare, scowling, presenting a clear physical warning to Brachias, despite his injuries.

"We're not prisoners!..."

Dienkes, Eurytus, and Alpheus all gather around Leonidas.

"We have a deal arranged with Lord Melech that involves an agreed upon fee of two years of military service from me and my men..."

Brachias's face sinks, and his eyes grow sad, shaking his head, sighing to no one.

"Not all prisoners wear chains..."

Brachias walks over towards one of the orbs and enters a series of inputs onto a small holo-keyboard projecting out from an adjacent column.

The machine under the orb begins to hum; bubbles rise within the orb as it floats between the machines like an alien sea creature.

Brachias gestures towards the orb with his thumb, smiling at the Spartans.

"Alright! Who's up first?!..."

SPARTANS IN SPACE 01

Alpheus sneers at the orb, jeering at Brachias, crossing both arms in front of him.

"Hmf.. What do you want us to do?..."

"?..."

Brachias studies the blank stares, stubborn looks, and stoic expressions across the Spartans' faces.

"Ha-ha!

I take it, none of you have ever tried one of these before?" Brachias says, pointing at the orb.

"So, you can just think of this as your very own personal swimming pool.

The liquid don't go nowhere because of the way it's designed .

You just step right in—and float!

The oxygen rich liquid keeps you from drowning, and its regenerative properties are what get you coming out of it feeling good as new!"

Brachias spots Leonidas eye-balling a body inside an orb.

"Most of us sleep while we're in 'em since there's barely enough room to do anything else."

Leonidas turns his head and studies Brachias...

"In any case,

closing your eyes and sleeping is a lot better than keeping them open and seeing everything all blurry and filtered blue.

But that's entirely up to you guys.

Y'all ain't injured too badly.

You should be good for about an hour."

His instincts tell him Brachias is trustworthy,

and so Leonidas steps forward, limping with his chin up, towards the sphere...

Leonidas frowns inquisitively at the orb, standing across from it.

And what does risk have in store for me now?...

Leonidas reaches his arm out, allowing it to pass through the orb, and watches as it floats between the thick cobalt-blue membrane.

I'm beginning to feel what that stone creature was talking about...

Removing his hand from inside the orb, Leonidas examines both sides of it.

The swelling on my hand has gone down...
How about that.

Turning towards his men with a grin brisk with mischief, Leonidas plunges himself into the sphere.

Floating freely inside the orb, Leonidas watches Brachias lead the other three Spartans and show them how to get into an orb of their own...

Leonidas's body is hugged by a warm sensation that forces every nerve in his body to suddenly relax.

Bubbles rise, and he floats weightless, crossing his arms as his knees bend pressed together, legs slowly shifting upwards towards his chest.

Hmf... This is the first chance I've had to relax since we've arrived.

As Leonidas's mind begins to settle, he feels the reality of it all gradually start to sink in.

All that is going on.

All that has happened.

And all the uncertainty of things to come.

So many thoughts at one time tires his mind,

and Leonidas chuckles at the ridiculousness of it all.

Too occupied in his own mind to notice himself falling asleep, the Spartan king closes his eyes and smiles as he floats—dreaming of home on an alien world—in a time not his own...

15

Weeks Pass...

And the Spartans have since been put on assignment.
"Finish conquering the people of Draman-TU and force them to bow down to the will of Argoss," Were the orders given by Melech before they left.
Leonidas sits on a long metal bench inside of a large carry-on ship as part of a burgeoning armada on its way to invade...
Brachias sits across from him, sharpening his ax, as well as a dozen others inside a large cabin with hundreds of more warriors of all shapes and sizes.
Each being wields his or her preferred weapon, and all sit, stand, sleep, or chit-chat as they all wait to arrive and

conclude the campaign of invading Draman-TU.

Brachias's eyes gleam as he sharpens his weapon.

"I take no pleasure in this, you know," he says, his eyes narrowing on the blade.

"Running up on a people I don't know and taking everything that belongs to them.

This was never part of the plan, if you had asked me, growing up. "

"Then why are you here?" Leonidas jeers, tilting his head, smiling crookedly as one eye tightens, locking sights on Brachias.

"Judging by the way you take to that weapon of yours, I'd say that you're eager to land on this planet and use it on the first person that gets in your way.

A little early to try and gain sympathy for your actions, don't you think?

You have to wait until *after* the deed before you go around pretending you feel bad about it."

Brachias meets Leonidas's gaze with a perturbed stare lined with vexation.

"Nice armor..." Brachias says.

"The Etherians on board make it for you?"

Alpheus and several other Spartans sit alongside Leonidas, killing time as they wait in brand new battle wears...

"Yes, and I must say I grow more and more impressed by their technical know-how..."

Each Spartan sits enveloped in brand new leg armor. Wrapping all the way up from the toes and around the waist, it shines with a solid, tempered, kevlar-black, over an Etherian labored interior laden with an iridescent array of biometric enhancing cybernetics designed to amplify leg performance.

Each Spartan's torso piece and helmet blazes with a raw

cyber-gold luster.

Their helmets maintain the original Greek designs displayed inside pages of the Magnus Compendium.

Leonidas's helmet differs from his men's, maintaining a smooth transition up from the front, in place of the jagged, stark point coming up on the others'.

Rounded shields lean peacefully at the knee of each of the men's sides.

Three-hundred and one Spartan swords gleam with lethal sheen in their hands, and Leonidas places his over his lap, continuing talking to Brachias.

"Yes,

with this armor I should have no trouble staying alive long enough to complete the deal fixed between Melech and myself."

"There you go with that deal again," Brachias says, flipping his ax over and sharpening it.

"What kind of deal did you end up cutting with Lord Melech, anyways?..."

Leonidas proceeds to tell Brachias everything,

about Sparta,

about the battle of Thermopylae,

about how him and his men lost their lives there,

and their eventual resurrection.

Leonidas highlights the terms should he ever want to see his friends and family again...

Sitting amongst the variable caterwauling inside the cabin,

Brachias looks at the floor after listening, in contemplative silence.

"...I really hate to break it to you," he says.

"But you're never going to see your friends and family again."

The words hit like a pin needle in the thigh, and Leonidas
glares sharply at Brachias.

"What do you mean?..."

Brachias turns his head to one side, sighs, before reply
back to Leonidas in a low, reserved tone.

"Twelve years ago, Argoss had commissioned my people to complete a huge mining project for them on planet
Reev...

The job was simple enough:

unearth all the precious mineral deposits from the soil
there and load it up onto transport carriers to be processed...

The precious minerals would be turned into weapons,
gems, tools,

you know,

things like that...

I come from Norev.

Our reputation for producing some of the universe's best
miners is well known amongst planets.

The job was contracted for five years, and we were en-
couraged to bring our families along to come live with us
in the new domestic housing settlements Argoss had just
built exclusively for the workers...

A lot of us said yes,

and the day finally came when all of Argoss's ships would
return to Norev and take us all to what would become our
home for the next five years.

I should probably point out that at this time rumors of
Argoss's cruelty hadn't yet spread to our part of the solar
system.

We all pretty much saw them as little more than snooty
contractors willing to pay up front...

Inside the ship I was on, accommodations consisted of
grouping us all in cramped rooms, sitting pressed against

each other, with our kids crying from the lack of space and terrible food.

As I sat there in that room, I looked over at my wife who knelt next to my two boys and could tell by the look in her eye that she had begun to regret coming here...

She didn't have the heart to saything, but I knew.

And seeing her suffer in silence like that only made me want to get up and do something about it.

I headed towards the exit.

And as I tried walking out of the room,

I was stopped by two really big guards posted outside the door.

You should have heard the way they talked to me.

'Woah woah woah!' one said.

'What can we do for you, hmm...?!'

Their attitude came as a bit of a shock and it put me slightly on edge.

'I have a complaint to make about the accommodations. The room is too small, and the food you've given us is tainted.

It can barely be *called* food at all.

Who can I go to about this?'

Those two guards looked at me like I was a child.

'That would be the captain you'd take your complaint to.'

'Yes, but right now the captain is very busy, I'm afraid.'

'Very busy.'

I could tell by the way they were looking at me that they weren't going to let me pass,

and so I walked back to my wife and kids, listening to the guards talk about me and laughing loud enough to make sure I could hear them.

My wife looked at me as I sat down, trying to put a smile in front of her grief, and I vowed to myself that I'd break out later that night, find the captain, and tell him about the food and room we've been forced to all cram in.

I thought the captain would reprimand the staff and fix everything.

Now,

fighting is something that comes naturally to all life,

but,

when my people do it,

it comes off a little bit more *explosive* thanks to our hard exterior...

Later that night, I convinced a couple of guys to pretend to get into it in order to generate a disturbance so I could sneak out.

It worked.

Treading through the halls, I put everything I had into trying to walk lightly and avoid being seen.

I didn't know what I was looking for.

Maybe some sort of hint or clue that would shed some light on where the captain was.

Walking down one hall, I heard footsteps coming towards me and so I backtracked and turned a corner and stopped and waited hoping the footsteps weren't planning on turning at the corner I was at.

I leaned against one side of the wall, and held my breath and listened as two guards walked past.

I could hear them talking about Reev, and the plans that Argoss had in store for us once we got there...

'I'm telling you, you're far better off *making* them work for us from the start rather than feeding them a dumb line about having them contracted for five years.'

'Scylus likes to mess with their heads.

He gets some kind of strange kick off manipulating people.

He's an absolute loon if you ask me.'

'No kidding.

Just makes you glad we fell into this gig instead of being shipped off to Reev with the rest of those poor bastards.'
'I heard that.
You know one of them tried complaining earlier.'
'About what?'
'Something about the size of the room and the kind of food they're getting.
Heard even a fight broke out.'
'Ha!
Yeah and I bet the poor idiot is finally realizing what he should have ought to by now!'
'That there is no mining job.'
'One that pays, anyways.'
'And that five years stands for a lifetime of servitude to Argoss.'
Ahahahahahahahahahahaha!!!'
I lost feeling in my fingertips, and my legs felt weak.
I felt nauseous, and thought I was going to throw up at any moment.
My mind started racing.
I had to get my family out of there before arriving on Reev.
I didn't know what to do but knew I couldn't just stand there and wait to get caught.
And then it hit me.
Most large ships like the one I was on have hangars in them that house a number of small exploratory crafts used for reconnaissance missions.
If I could just commandeer one of them,
then it could be me and my family's ticket out of there.
I first had to find the hangar,
then, slink my way back to the room,
grab my wife and kids,
sneak them back *out* of the room,

and scramble back to the hangar with them without ever being seen.

The whole thing seemed doomed from the start.

Finding the hangar was easy enough, I just made my way down through the ship's lower levels and moved through the different floors until I finally ran across it.

There were only a handful of soldiers occupying it at the time, so I managed to sneak in without raising any suspicion...

Hiding behind large cargo crates stacked high on top of each other, I carefully scanned the hangar for an ideal ship for me and my wife.

My best bet laid in a small, yellow and black two-seater model lying at the edge of the hangar, closest to the launch gate .

A two-seater would mean me and my wife would have to double up with the kids,

but,

considering the direness of the circumstances,

convenience would have to take a back seat to urgency.

16

"I left the hangar soon after choosing the ship I wanted, and headed back to the room.
Harboring a flood of different emotions, I found it hard to step lightly to avoid being seen.
I almost had a panic attack.
Before I knew it, I was looking out from the edge of a corner, only a few feet away from the two guards outside the room I was in with my wife and kids.
I had no idea on how to get past those guards.
I was beginning to worry I'd get noticed just standing around,
and so I thought and thought on a solution that would let me get past those guards without being seen...

With no immediate thoughts coming to mind, I decided to capitalize on *one* thing I knew, something made perfectly clear the very first time I spoke to those guards—
They didn't think much of me.
I emerged from the corner I was in and let myself be seen.
Raising my hands up, I casually approached the two guards.
'Well well well,' one said.
'What have we here?...'
'Looks like one got away during that little scuffle we had earlier.'
'Did you get lost?!'
The two guards took their time mocking me, calling me all types of names.
All the while I just stood there trying to figure out my next move.
'That's why it's better for you to stay in your room so we can keep an eye on you.'
The two leaned in close,
and we suddenly stood face-to-face.
'So what do you have to say for yourself, hmm?'
When people think they're better than you they don't see you as a threat, and are more inclined to act cool in front of you, which can be a little reckless.
Fueled by the image of my wife being forced to lie with my kids in that awful, cramped room, I clenched my fists and ran them into the heads of both of those guards as hard as I could.
The two of them never saw it coming.
Both the guards dropped, and I bypassed them, running into the room to grab my wife and two boys...
The others looked at me with surprise when they saw what I had done to both of the guards.
I tried to tell everyone what I had heard, and that they

needed to quickly follow me back to the hangar to have any chance at escape.

' .... '

Silence...

I don't know if it was because of fear, but, some of my people opted to stay.

Others said I was trying to sabotage the job because I was having second thoughts about working five years, away from home.

In any case, I couldn't let them stand in my way.

I was going to escape either with or without them, with both my wife and kids.

The four of us rushed down to the ship's lower levels.

Turning a corner, we were startled by an alarm I could only guess meant someone had stumbled onto the two guards I laid out.

With the sound of the alarm, I threw caution to the wind, and both me, my wife and kids ran frantically through halls and around corners, certain the ship was already searching for us.

When we finally got to the hangar, I suddenly realized something that I had missed.

Something that didn't dawn on me until I was there a second time.

How the hell do I get the launch gate to open?!!

I immediately looked at my wife,

her eyes were wide and she was shaking.

There was no way I was going to lead my family all the way down here just so we could get caught and brought back.

I quickly showed my wife the ship I had chosen, and she immediately hopped in the cockpit along with our two boys.

I set coordinates on the ship for the nearest star system

before running back to a large control panel on the opposite side of the hangar.

I was certain that *this* had to operate the launch gate.

There were so many knobs, buttons, and switches, all I could do was take my time trying to decipher them through that damned alarm.

I could hear the sounds of guards closing in on the large door of the hangar, which I managed to seal after getting in.

As I was finally starting to get a feel for all the switches and knobs, the entrance door behind me suddenly came crashing down.

It was like a sea of armed guards pouring in.

And all of them stood around the entrance to the hangar.

Out of time, my fingers just *went*.

And I clicked, flipped, and twisted switches, knobs, and buttons at random hoping to get lucky off a whim and trigger the launch gate to open.

Well,

as luck would have it,

the launch gate engaged.

And I stood there flabbergasted after seeing it slowly start opening.

Then the armed guards started firing...

I ran through the weapon fire towards my wife and two kids.

And I watched as their screams were made mute by the ammo riddling the ship I had chosen.

Closing in on the ship, I looked at the gate, realizing there would be dozens of ships coming after us as soon as we cleared it...

Anxious to make a deal with fate in favor of my wife, I smiled as I reached the ship, and my family hugged me despite everything being torn apart around us.

I'll never forget that.

Time went slow for me then, as I looked at my family, and I could no longer hear the sound of the weapon fire despite seeing it everywhere.

I closed the cockpit latch above them and yelled 'Go!'

motioning my wife towards the open gate,

and watched my sons scream, and yell for me to go with them as I turned my back to all three.

Turning my back to them then, I became someone on a mission.

Nothing was going to stop me if it was to help my family get away.

The first thing I did as I walked back was rip the wheel off a small ship adjacent to me and chucked it hard at another ship, filling the whole left side of the hanger with a bellowing, monstrous flame.

The beams from the guards' weapons smashed into me, which, because of my tough hide, honestly didn't do much.

I slammed my arm through the heart of another ship, triggering an explosion in that one as well.

The guards were yelling curses at me as I looked back to see my wife finally reaching for life, deciding to take off.

'Stop her!!!'

one guard yelled, but I threw large chunks of hot metal, damaging ships and congesting the launch track, scattering guards in the process trying to avoid being hit.

They all charged at me then, but I stood my ground, and the sounds of their beams were replaced with charged screams from the hundreds of them now quickly closing in...

The bravest of them reached me first, and I grabbed him by the neck and threw him at the next batch following behind.

I don't remember saying a word, but I remember the effect my eyes had on them as I handled one,

and another one,

and another one,

and another one!

all in bitter, relentless thrashing.

It all feels a little unreal looking back on it now.

The guards thought they could overwhelm me with their numbers, but I stayed as more and more came, and all I could do was try and stay focused on buying my wife enough time for her and our kids to escape.

I felt the pull from hundreds of hands grabbing me all at once,

pulling me down along with the weight from the rest of the guards as they piled up on top of me...

My knees started to buckle under the constant strain of their effort, and for a moment I thought that was it for me.

I held on to the image of my wife in my head, and knew that I had to make it out of this if I ever wanted to see her again.

At that moment, I found the will to keep going, and rose up with enough force to send all the guards on top of me flying.

I was breathing heavy, watching the guards scattered, knowing they'd recover any minute now to continue their assault on me.

Not wanting to wait, I grabbed a large chunk of metal and held it with both hands, charging forward, yelling, towards the guards who were just beginning to bounce back.

'Rahhhrgh!!!'

As the gap between us began closing,

I heard a deep voice call out to me from someone standing at the entrance to the hangar.

'While I do admire your tanacity!' the voice said,

'I simply cannot allow you to go any farther!...'

I forgoed my charge and turned around, following the voice.

Which led my eyes to Scylus, standing between two large guards half machine, half beast from somewhere I've never seen with large horns on their heads.

Those things were armored thick, and some people think I'm huge, heh...

Mind you, I didn't know Scylus was captain at the time, but by the way he made the rest of the guards stop what they were doing, I could tell at least that he had to be someone important.

'C-Captain Scylus,' one of the guards next to me muttered out, which flipped my switch back into rage mode on an entirely new target.

My nostrils flared, and my teeth gnashed as I cracked the floor with a step and charged towards Scylus with everything I had.

I now knew that his lies are what got my family into this mess.

I gripped the large chunk of metal in my hand so tight that my fingers began to warp it, as I steadily closed the distance between me and Scylus.

He didn't even try to move.

In that instant,

just as I'm about to pile down on Scylus with everything I have, one of his guards steps in wielding a rod that strikes me and sends my mind screaming as every nerve inside me is pumped full of electricity.

'Arghharghhgharghhghhghh!!!

N-Noooo...'

I barely got those words out as my body went down.

It takes both those guards that Scylus brought to lift me up, and I stood there disoriented, seeing doubles of everything...

Scylus looked up and studied me before looking around at the hangar.

I could tell he wasn't happy.

Scylus then looked over to a couple of guards, gesturing towards *me*.

The guards proceeded to place me in shackles and remove me from the hangar...

I spent three weeks after that living in isolation, exercising in a pitch-black cell, eating the horrible food that they gave me.

All I could think about were the whereabouts of my family, and whether or not they managed to make it out okay...

It wasn't until the fourth week that I found out I wouldn't be joining the rest of my people on Reev.

And that my little stunt had instead garnered me a spot in the arena.

I have been competing in matches on Argoss ever since."

Leonidas stares at Brachias with unanswered curiosity.

"I never saw them again,

My family.

It's been twelve years.

Since then, I still have a gut feeling that they're still out there somewhere waiting for me.

That's why I can't die yet.

Not yet...

Not until I find my wife and kids,

and find a place for us to live away from Argoss's influence.

Until then, it's hell to pay for all those who get in my way..."

Leonidas smirks at the bold statement, and stands offering an arm in friendship to the large stone warrior.

"Well then good luck to you," he says.

"May fate smile on your journey until you reach its end." The two of them share a warrior's handshake, exchanging sharp glances, before the entire ship is alive with red lights everywhere and a shrieking siren.

REEEEEEEEEOOOOHHREEEEEEEEOOOOOHH!
REEEEEEEEEOOOOHHREEEEEEEEOOOOOHH!

A loud voice rings over an intercom attached to the ceiling.

"Coming up on Draman-TU!
All soldiers gear up!"

The voice is met with a change in atmosphere, as Leonidas and the rest of those on the ship begin securing their weapons, getting ready for battle.

"Looks like this is it," Brachias says, adjusting the massive plate armor over his shoulder.

"Are you all ready?..."

Leonidas unearths a cunning smirk, looking over towards his men.

"Spartaaaaanns...!!

Are you ready?!"

Haroooh!! Haroooh!!
Haroooh!! Haroooh!!!

The cabin rattles with a singular voice, as Brachias looks at Leonidas and nods with approval,

"Hrmff!"

Gripping his ax with both hands, Brachias stands high as he looks to one side and boldly declares...

"Let's do this..."

17

Hundreds of ships arrive off the shores of a massive lake at the center of a large meadow blessed with stretches of rich grassland...

Gentle waves crash, and the air hisses with the fizz from the water that shoots up towards the blue sky overseeing the ships as they land.

A cool breeze swirls through the warm air, filling it with the *wisshhh* from the leaves rustling amongst alien fruit from the neighboring trees.

The tranquility of the area is almost palpable.

A living portrait of nature in constant flux, changing along with all the transient wildlife that enters its borders...

The ships lay over the water like rows of massive insects sleeping in colonies, piercing the serenity of the landscape with their deep mechanical groans...

SLAM! SLAM! SLAM! SLAM! SLAM! SLAM! SLAM!

Large ramps on the backs of the ships slam down against the shore, kicking up clumps of wet sand as thousands of warriors quickly begin to pile out.

Stepping out onto the shore, Leonidas immediately notices the similarities of this place and Earth.

"Hmf...

Looks almost like home..."

The clear, jewel-blue sky,

the aurora-green trees,

and the air, so clean, rejuvenates Leonidas's lungs as he steps from the sand to the mainland, breathing it in.

"Krooooh-ahh..."

Joined by his men, the Spartans gather among the horde of other warriors from the collection of ships.

The massive colorful army hums coarsely from conversation, standing idly waiting for orders from Scylus who has yet to emerge from a ship.

Looking fondly at the grass, Leonidas's eyes rise towards the sky, and he sighs as the breeze brings with it a comforting draft from memory.

"Wish it *was* home..."

Accompanied by a team of four officers, Scylus emerges from a ship.

Standing, making his presence known at the top of the ramp, Scylus aims his nose high as his arms cross pompously behind him.

"...."

Wrapped in gorgeous black, purple, and gold battle gear,

draped by a silk-like, metallic cloak, Scylus gradually lowers his head and surveys the lot of warriors standing about.

Scylus irksomely looks over the bunch as they converse, unsheathing a screech piercing the ears of all.

"Iiiarrrrrghhh!!!"

!!?

......

...

..

Scylus adopts a pretentious grin and steps forward.

"I suppose I should thank you all for coming," he says. "But,

as you know...

Fighting for Argoss is a privilege and reward all unto itself..."

The lot of warriors look up at the honcho, sneering, exhibiting warped smiles and eyes highlighting their bitterness...

"All of you know why you have been ordered to come here!" Scylus says.

"To the east of here lies the last populated city that remains on this planet!

And yet...

Despite witnessing the fall of their neighbors,

its inhabitants continue to hold on to their ridiculous beliefs, denying the truth and salvation that comes from aligning oneself with Argoss...

In one hour we will set off for the city!

and administer that which befalls those who go against the rule of Lord Melech!

I expect you all to be ready by then..."

Scylus grabs his cloak and it flaps as he turns and goes
back into the ship with his four officers.
"Was that supposed to be a speech?!" Alpheus quips,
curling his lip up at where Scylus was standing.
"Hmf!
So what now?" Alpheus says, turning to Leonidas.
Leonidas crosses his arms and closes his eyes, crossing
his legs as he plants himself down on the grass.
"We wait..."

A brisk breeze stirs the trees, and seconds sail to minutes
as Leonidas basks on the grass, eating fruit that has fallen,
surveying the surrounding nature.
"Can't say I blame the inhabitants for wanting to fight for
this planet."
The warm rays from the sun warms Leonidas's face, and
he leans back to relax as the shade from something passing completely envelops him.
Leonidas opens one eye, spying Scylus driving a large
vehicle with spikes, small turrets, and flames *spurting* out
from all sides.
"...."
Hovering low to the ground, the large vehicle is soon
accompanied by four more of its kind, driven by Scylus's
four officers.
The four ride through the mob of warriors as they clear a
path for them, stopping just short from the edge of a hill
twenty two yards from the beach.
Scylus looks out from the edge of the hill, gauging the
distance between him and a beautiful city standing another hundred yards beyond.
"How I can taste you..."
Scylus licks his lips, producing a black, mid-sized, metallic bar lined with symbols and grooves, from underneath

his cloak.

Scylus drops his arms and sighs, eyeballing the city as a bright light suddenly *bursts* from the top of the bar, revealing a red and imposing beam saber.

CHZYZYZYZYZYZYZYZYZ!

The saber incinerates the air around it.

Leonidas looks on, enrapt by the weapon.

Scylus raises his saber and grins, looking back at the warriors as his entire face contorts with malevolent intent...

"Let's go..."

Lurking beyond the edge of the field stands the last populated city of Draman-TU.

With majesty and complexity distributed in equal parts, its buildings rise like sparkling peaks over winding roads and city blocks sectioned off by novel application of complex geometry.

It's a towering bejeweled maze.

Inside,

its red-fleshed inhabitants adopt crimson robes in remembrance of the bloodshed in defiance to Argoss.

Above the streets,

posted in towers,

warriors lurk in red capes draped over armor as black as cauldrons.

To all that live within the city gates, the day goes on like any other:

quiet;

with the smog of fear and uncertainty blowing its haze over all.

Everyone lives ever worried if today will be the day that brings with it the next invasion...

A frail marketplace operates in a midtown district, and patrons visit it insistent on a scrap of normality.
A child stands idle as her mother peruses through jewelry, Ooooing the two light trails sailing high in the sky over-head.

SMASH!!SMASH!!

The child's golden eyes widen, delighting in the light trails colliding vibrantly with the side of a nearby build-ing.

"Prettyyyy..."

The sky over the marketplace glistens with glass and jagged debris as it falls meeting the rising screams from patrons running for their lives.
The guards on the towers look down towards the street—then back up! as their attention is stolen by the faint *hiss* caused by Argoss's warriors shouting as they all come charging towards the city, far off in the distance.
Scylus leads the charge of gold and shimmering plate gleaming amongst the horde as it comes pouring across the field like an unstoppable plague.
Scylus raises his beam saber up high and smiles wildly as the spikes on his vehicles stick out more,
and the flames blowing from all sides of it singe the air...

18

The sky turns gray as the clouds come in, bringing with
them flashes of lightning that illuminate the field.
KRI-CLASHHH!!!
The rain pours down as Argoss's horde moves closer,
and Leonidas looks at the sky, wondering what it means...
As Scylus and his men keep gaining more ground, details
of the city gradually start growing clearer and clearer.
Coming on thirty yards from the city gates, Leonidas
looks up as the clouds over the city slowly begin to break
revealing one star,
and another,
and another,
and another!

until the entire sky is littered with their orange-red glint...
As Scylus and the horde close in, the stars in the sky
gradually shift, and all start plummeting down towards
him and his men.
As the entire sky seems to be falling down on them,
from the city soldiers from Draman-TU suddenly come
storming out through the gates!
"Here they come!" Scylus shouts.
"Kill them!
Kill them all!!!..."

Coming up on foot and one man hover cruisers, the warriors of Draman-TU charge fiercely to meet the warriors
from Argoss.

Both sides *smash!* in a massive clash, setting off a congested storm of weapons swinging in a dense mix of
chaos...
the entire field gasps with carnage and confusion—
made worse by the sudden appearance of the falling stars
as they finally touch down.

CRASHCRASHCRASHCRASHCRASHCRASHCRASH!!!

Leonidas and others from both sides are scattered as the
hot projectiles touch down.
Scrambling back to his feet,
Leondias looks on, and sees that the stars are in fact pulse
blasts sent from turrets positioned on top of buildings
inside the city.
The stars kick up hunks of dirt, creating small craters as
their bludgeoning blitzkrieg relentlessly rains down on
top of warriors from Argoss and Draman-TU alike...
Amid the mix of pulse blasts, weapons clashing, and

forest of screams, one of those on hover cruiser sets his sights on a distracted Leonidas...

As Leonidas swings his sword inside the cramped quarters of the congested battlefield, he fails to notice the hover cruiser now obsessively rushing towards him.

Its rider's eyes home in on Leonidas, as his scarlet cape flaps over the couldron-black armor...

Blocking an attack from another warrior forces Leonidas to turn,

noticing the enemy rushing towards him, from the corner of his eye.

"Hmf!"

Leonidas is void of options.

"That thing he's riding is liable to catch me no matter which direction I run."

As the cruiser closes in, Leonidas leaps at the last second, extending his sword forward, skewering the rider's core... The force of the blow sends the rider falling backwards off the vehicle.

The rider gasps and convulses, coughing up blood as Leonidas stands over him smirking in the heart of the mayhem.

"Good *try*..."

Leonidas pulls his sword from the rider's core, and uses it to sever the rider's cape, draping it over his own armor.

"Only Spartans can wear crimson on the battlefield."

Holding tightly to his sword and shield, Leonidas turns from the dying warrior and charges boldly back into the thick of battle...

19

The fighting carries on until late in the day with neither side relinquishing an *inch* to the other.
While one side fights to preserve its freedom, the other side fights to preserve the little freedome it already has.
In the end, the warriors of Draman-TU lay fallen, and Argoss stands victorious, as the black sky rains down on another conquered planet.
There are no survivors...
The rain has turned the battlefield to mud that has partially buried the bodies of countless others that lay scattered about.
Lightning strikes over the dark tranquility—
KRI-CLASHHH!!!

Leonidas sits on a stone and goes over the ordeal as he contemplates the day's events and sorts them out in his head.

Well at least the dynamics of war haven't changed much.
I ought to survive the next two years.

The rain rattles his helmet.

It stifles his thinking.

So he takes it off and sets it down on the ground beside him...

Leonidas stares out into nothing, taking it all in, as a flash of lightning illuminates the field and reveals the looming death toll around him...

KRI-CLASHHH!!!

"..?!"

Leonidas suddenly spots something odd not far in the distance.

Laying one with the mud, amongst the scores of deceased, a familiar arm slowly reaches up, shaking, barely clinging to life.

"No..."

Squinting his eyes, focusing, hoping they're both lying, Leonidas rises quickly and bolts it over to the poor soul lying in the mud.

The mix of shock and certainty inadvertently shortens his stride, as Leonidas closes in on a mortally wounded Alpheus.

"My King..."

The Spartan lays spread, half dead, with blood coming from the corner of his nose and mouth,

A half sword sticks out from between his ribs, and Leonidas kneels, giving Alpheus a once-over before removing his helmet.

The injured Spartan looks over and coughs, futilely, smiling, admiring Leonidas with death-clouded eyes.

"My Ki-ng..."
"Hush now.
There's no use draining your strength on one last good-
bye...
You fought well...
As reward for your courage, I order you to take an ex-
tended vacation for two years.
Use the time to visit your friends and family again.
Give them my regards."

"H-Heh...
As.. you wish..."

Alpheus turns his head back, looking up at the sky,
painfully placing one hand on his chest as his last breath
leaves his body...
The rain falls on both spartans, as fate reclaims one, taking him back to the afterlife.
Leonidas kneels with his eyes closed as the lighting
screams and wind howls under the hissing of the rain.
As he kneels, Leonidas feels his thoughts being constrict-
ed, conflicted—
drawing a blank as black as a sky without stars at night,
and everything feels like it's going dark around him.

"..."

"........"

Sometime later,

Scylus calls for his men to gather and meet him at the center of the field, where he plans to address everyone before heading back to the ships.

Leonidas sighs as he gets up, grabbing Alpheus's helmet.

As warriors gradually make their way towards the center of the field, Leonidas looks back at the remnants of the conquered city.

The city smolders, black, charred, battered, raped of all beauty and left to reflect by its lonesome as the perpetrators leave.

Mashing through mud and discarded weapons next to the endless un-alive, Leonidas meets up with other Spartans who got separated during the heat of battle.

"It's good to see you're still alive, my king,"

Eurytus says, with a left eye swollen almost as shut as the severed one.

Carrying a cracked ax, a tired limp, and chips over both of his eyes, Brachias smiles as he spots Leonidas and his men walking towards him, at the center of the field.

"'T's good to see you didn't die on your first assignment,"

Brachias joshes, his eyes blazing playfully, in the thick of the mud.

"Be quiet!" Leonidas admonishes.

"Casualties in war are to be expected.

It makes no difference if you died fighting or not so long as you fought well!"

Leonidas turns his head, reflecting, thinking of Alpheus...

As the majority of warriors arrive at the center of the field,

Scylus appears with his four officers, steering their vehicles into the middle of the crowd.

Scylus stands up and steps on top of his vehicle.

"Well done!"

Scylus says, stretching his arms out, calling out to all within earshot of his voice.

"Today you have all honored yourselves by working together to eliminate a very dangerous enemy of the Argoss empire.

Lord Melech be praised because without his vision for the cosmos we may have never recognized the evil of these people whose ways are so different they pretty much called us here to punish them..."

The warriors share perturbed glances at Scylus's claims.

"However!...

No army is that without its commanders and so I want you all to thank your four chief superior officers for helping to give you all this victory today.

I don't have to remind you that one does not have to be in your presence for our presence to affect you all effectively."

Thank you sirs!!!

The words belch out bitterly from the majority of warriors.

"A second team will eventually return here to collect all articles of value!

When I give word,

I want you all to pick yourselves up and follow me back to the ships.

The resident Etherians there will all tend to your wounds and treat them all according to their severity.

You should all be very proud of yourselves today.

For your efforts, each of you shall receive an extra portion of food in this months rations, following our return

to Argoss...
Dismissed!"

The lot of warriors churn and groan, initiating the exhausted trudge back to the ships.

I have to know!...

Leonidas grinds his teeth and takes off,
traversing the sum of the exodus, reaching the front led
by Scylus and his four officers.
"Scylus!
A word with you please!"
Walking side-by-side with the lead spiked vehicle,
Leonidas looks up beyond the clumps of caked on, blood-
stained mud, watching Scylus riding poised, not visually
acknowledging him.
 "Oh, Leonidas.
What can I do for you?"
"Alpheus is dead,"
"Oh...
What a pity," Scylus cites, sarcastically...
"I want your word that you're going to bring him back
with the other Spartans at the end of the two years!"
"And why would I do that, my dear boy?"
" *Eh,* Because we have a deal, that's why!"
"I never said I'd bring back the Spartans who died after
they were already brought back.
Just the ones who already died back on *your* planet, was
our arrangement.
Besides...
That troublesome wretch was bound to die by someone's
hand sooner or later.
It's just a shame I couldn't be there to witness it for my-

self..."

Leonidas steps back, as the caravan continues,
slack-jawed and small pupiled,
his left hand clenched and shaking.

"..! ....! .!"

"Oh hey, it's you!"

"huh?"

Leonidas looks down to the sound of a small voice and
sees a bloodied Etherian smiling strenuously, with a hard
limp and a robot arm.

Halting his stride and wincing, holding his side, the Etherian grips a slash made through his light, high-tech armor.

"*Ngh!* I always wondered what happened to you.
I saw some of your kind out here in the battle."

Leonidas Pivots his head, squinting, trying to find out
where he might know this Etherian from...

"I doubt that you'd've remembered me.
I was one of the ones who worked on your resurrection
before the Xarcon Crystal blew up."

Xarcon Crystal?...

Leonidas thinks back, recalling the massive diamond and
machine that brought him and his men back from the
dead...

"So what are you doing here?
I thought Etherians Don't believe in Violence..."

"*Ngh!..* Heh, I suppose you're right, *Ngh!...*

But,
this is punishment for refusing to conduct autopsies on
living subjects for Argoss.

Ngh! The Irony isn't lost on me.

'Least the subjects have the chance to defend themselves
here.

In any case,
After the Xarcon gem blew, we had the Transmutation

Matrix stripped for parts and weren't sure what Scylus
had in store for you and your kind.
It's good to see you're still living.
Keep it up.
Sooner or later we'll all find a way to escape Argoss's
reach.
'Just have to keep our eyes and ears open...'
With one final wince, the Etherian limps on, joining the
groaning, trudging caravan back to the ships.
Stripped for parts?
Leonidas stands vexed,
perplexed,
sojourned,
dreading,
and the words of a perturbed Cerix manifest themselves
in his head.

Scylus had never intended to do what he said!
This existence is exactly what he had in store for us!

"No..."

Leonidas grabs the back of his neck, remembering the
words Brachias had said to him prior.

Not all prisoners wear chains...

You're never going to see your friends and family again.

"This is insane!"

Leonidas grinds his teeth;
Looking down.
Brandishing fist; breathing heavily,

SPARTANS IN SPACE 01

trembling,
disassociated from everything else around him.

That troublesome wretch was bound to die by someone's hand sooner or later...

It's just a shame I couldn't be there to witness it for myself.

Scylus's words invade Leonidas's psyche,
and Leonidas grabs his head, as everything around him
suddenly goes into a violent, chaotic spin.

Leonidas calls to his men, grabbing firm to reality, quelling the spin.

"Spartans, halt!!!"

The drudgery of the trudging caravan comes to a halt, and all the warriors hand blank stares and scared glances back at an intense, distressed, and hyperventilating Leonidas...

"What's going on back there?!" turns an irked, sore, and irate Scylus.
Leonidas's teeth gnash, calling his brow to furrow, looking back at Scylus with the utmost conviction.
"My men and I are staying here."
"What...?"
Scylus's face gnarls with distaste, getting up and standing at the top of his vehicle.
"You can't take spoils with you Leonidas!
All articles of value are immediately seized and used to fund numerous operations throughout the empire.
Were you not listening before?"
"Perfectly...
But we're still staying here..."
A mist of whispers wisp up like spores amongst the warriors, responding to Leonidas's strife-filled words.
"I don't understand," Scylus says.
"And what about the Spartans left to be revived?
Will you be turning your back on them as well?.."
"I... don't even know if it's possible to revive them any more..."
Leonidas looks at his trembling hand clenched in front of him, viewing all the cuts and scrapes made on it so far.
"You refuse to revive Alpheus.
And the only excuse you can provide is that it wasn't part of our agreement...
Our agreement was for you to bring back Sparta."
Swiping the air to one side, Leonidas raises Alpheus's helmet in front of him, aiming it at Scylus.
"What point is there in fighting to see our loved ones

again when our own death is what keeps us from being revived along with them?!"

Listening as he squints one eye, Scylus crosses his arms, standing at the top of his vehicle as Leonidas's words pervade throughout the field.

"Changing the terms of our agreement because you don't like Alpheus is petty.

I can only imagine you'll try doing it again the next time a Spartan does something you don't like.

I can't risk the lives of my men on a deal that doesn't suit them, much less one made with someone prone to childish whims.

Our pact is hereby rendered null and void, Scylus.

Tell Melech my men and I all died in battle...."

Leonidas turns, walking back towards the city as Spartans gradually begin sifting out from the crowd to follow.

Scylus grinds his teeth as he stares into Leonidas with jagged, cutting eyes...

"You think you can just tell yourself what to do?...

I own you, Leonidas!!!"

Raising his eyebrows, squinting his eyes, Leonidas turns his head left partways towards Scylus

"I wonder...

What could you do if everyone here suddenly decided they weren't going to take orders from you anymore?.."

Posture drawn straight as his jaw parts, eyes widen and shake, and Scylus Listens to the springing of quiet chatter suddenly emanating amongst the warriors.

Scowling with hate, Scylus aims his index finger at the back of Leonidas's head.

"Two years!..

A two year respite from all duty to the first one who can eliminate the Spartan!"

A thousand *what, wows,* and *gasps* inhabit the field, and

Leonidas stands finding himself surrounded by warriors.

" ....."

Scanning the horde encircling him, circling, with a firm grip on his sword, Leonidas glares at all, preparing for battle.

As Leonidas has his back turned to a section of the crowd, a zealous warrior suddenly leaps forward to lay claims on the prize.

"Hiargggggh!!!"

ZLASH!!!

...

A body drops, and all goes mute, as at the center of the horde stands Brachias with his ax held, over the Zealous warrior.

The crowd jolts and writhes with a mix of tension and fear as Brachias's eyes blaze at them all with roaring judgment.

Raising his chin, holding his ax lower some, Brachias looks over the crowd.

"Now, I don't know about you,
but I'm sick of Argoss thinking it can do what it wants with us!...

Leonidas is right!...

Who would Argoss send if all the warriors decided they weren't going to fight anymore?!

Seems like Argoss needs us more than we need them!

A fresh start here holds more promise than anything found back on the ships.

I'm staying too,
and I encourage you all to join!"

A myriad of awkward glances exchange among the rumbling of hundreds of convos suddenly going on amongst the warriors.

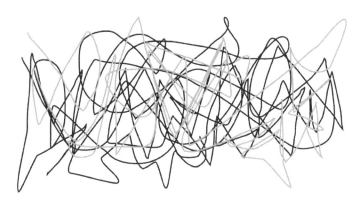

"Quiettt...!!!"

......

The warriors gradually settle down, and all is a hiss, parting for Scylus and his four officers driving towards Leonidas.
"I don't believe the lot of you! Scylus scolds.
None of you has any say in where you may go!
Idiots!
I'll see to it your rations all get cut in half for failing to act accordingly when ordered, and entertaining talk of mutiny...."

The warriors contract, rankled by Scylus's words, serving bitter glances back and forth at him and four officers.

"Now," Scylus says, parked one with the warriors making up the edge of the inner circle surrounding Leonidas.

I want you to kill Brachias, and Leonidas—
along with his men, for conspiring to raise upset and anarchy against the light shining Argoss,
and unending,
unyielding,
unfathomable hope inducing.
grand and illustrious will of Lord Melech!!!

Huff... Huff..."

...

20

Lightheaded and wild-eyed at the top of his vehicle,
Scylus feels the searing stares of a hundred thousand warriors glaring at him.
Scylus pants as his eyes jerk left and right, and a trail of
sweat trickles precariously down one side of his forehead.

"Don't just stand there, you fools!
  Do as I command!!!..."

....

SPARTANS IN SPACE 01

A heavy tension inhabits the air,
and Scylus swallows, panting heavier, looking sharply
around the field.

"Looks like they're not inclined to take orders from you
anymore..."

Scylus follows the voice and looks down to see Leonidas
standing across from him devil-grinned and fox-eyed.

"Hmf!
It seems like they've finally stumbled onto the truth.
I'm glad...
If me and my men are to rebuild here, an extra set of ap-
pendages is always welcome to help carry the load..."

Scylus gnashes his teeth, his eyes wide and beast-like.
"There will be no *load* for them to carry, other than the
weight of the world on their backs as theirs comes crashing down on them as soon as we get back to Argoss..."
Scylus reaches into his cloak, producing a red flash, and
Leonidas stands with the crimson beam saber aimed inches away from his nose.
Leonidas feels the heat from the intriguing blade as it
incinerates the air around it.

"Now, I don't know who you think you are," Scylus says.
But I'll be damned if let any of you remain here alive."

Leonidas scoffs at Scylus's comment.

"Heh, I still can't believe you haven't noticed it yet."

Writhing with rage at the vague critique, Scylus swings his sword vertically thrusting it closer to Leonidas.

"Noticed what?!.."
"Heh."
Leonidas shrugs his shoulders, stepping back, putting on Alpheus's helmet.
"Why not ask one of your men to tell you?
It's obvious they've already figured it out..."

"Don't play games with *me,* Leonidas!
There is nothing my men could know that I couldn't.
Nothing my men could do that would change their situation.
And nothing that any one of my men can say that will get me to Spare your life.
Now...
Do you really have something to tell me?
Or are you just stalling for time?..."

Leonidas grabs the back of his neck, flashing a sharp grin as he looks up.
"The truth is,
without a strong enough force to support it, an empire cannot thrive.
It would be completely obliterated by those with more power.
And so, just as Brachias said earlier, which,
even now remains true.
Without an army Argoss is nothing...
and neither are you."

Leonidas thrusts forward, drawing his sword, clashing with Scylus's as warriors rush in from all sides grabbing hold of Scylus's vehicle.

The four officers are smothered by the mob, and Scylus and them are rocked violently from side-to-side.

Scylus is panicked, slashing every which way as warriors start climbing the sides of his vehicle.

In a bout of desperation, Scylus goes into a spin, knocking those on his vehicle off as he accelerates forward.

The four officers follow desperately as Scylus races for the ships, launching bodies up high as he flies by making his way up the hill.

Watching Scylus getting away,

Leonidas raises his sword, roaring, as his eyes slice through the air.

"Spartanns!!!

Chaaaarge!!!"

The entire army casts off, going after Scylus, shouting wildly as he and his four officers race desperately towards the ships.

Above the hill, on the beach where the ships lay silently under the sway of trees, the serene scene is infiltrated by a faint,

HUSHHHHHHHHHHHH

far off in the distance...

Scylus and his four officers emerge up from the edge of the hill, followed by an amalgamation of curses and hollering only seconds behind them.

Gunning for the ships,

at the edge of the hill emerges one warrior,

then two,

then six!

followed by clumps of them running along the stream of the thousands more pouring up from the field.
The mob moves forward under unified hollering as they steadily close the distance between them and the ships.

Racing towards one of the large cargo ramps on the back of a ship, Scylus clips the incline coming up it, sending his vehicle flipping into the ceiling.

His four officers are not far behind...

Lying on the floor, Scylus quickly jumps to his feet, frantically sending word to those piloting the ship to take off immediately.

Desperate blasts release from the thrusters as they frantically engage, slowly raising the ship Scylus is in and zipping away haphazardly.

As the other ships begin to rise, the mob of warriors finally catch up to them.
Like a tribe of hunter gatherers in pursuit of a large beast, the warriors leap on top of the ships as they try to make their escape.
Over the lake, ships lean and tip, trying to shake as many warriors off of them as they can.
Like a colony of ants trying to devour a crab from the inside out, warriors race to get in through the open cargo ramps crew had desperately overlooked to quickly get going.

Arriving finally at the shore, throughout the tumultuous blitz, Leonidas looks up, spotting a ship disappearing far off in the distance.

"Damn..."

Turning his head towards the charged scene behind him,
Leonidas joins in the frenzied, allied pursuit of all of the
ships.
The beach lays embedded with the carcasses of ships, as
other ships tip, escaping, barely able to stay aloft.

Inside ships on the beach, warriors ransack every inch of
them, getting away with as much as they can carry while
simultaneously destroying any symbols or decorations
celebrating Argoss.
Walking in on the looting of a cargo bay, Leonidas remembers the Etherians onboard.
"Come on!"
Signaling to Brachias and five more, Leonidas and them
charge through the rank chaos, trying to locate the labs.
Darting down a dark hallway, bypassing dozens of rooms
filled with scientific equipment, Leonidas can tell by their
state that they've recently been occupied.
The six are met by a large industrial door at the end of the
hall, and Leonidas signals for Brachias to come over...

Huddled together on the other side of the door, a group
of Etherians tremble in fear, listening to the ruckus from
everything going on in the ship.

A series of loud strikes come from the door, and the
Etherians close their eyes, holding on tight to each other,
fearing the worst.

SMASH!... SMASH!!... SMASH!!... SMASH!!!!

Dust kicks up as the door comes down, and the Etherians wince seeing the motley crew of Leonidas, Brachias, and the other five warriors.

"Come with us!" Leonidas says in a warm, positive tone, outstretching his arm, gesturing for the Etherians to all come out of the room...
As the Etherians pile out, Leonidas recognizes Cerix among them.
Cerix spots Leonidas and stops, looking up at him.
"Leonidas?...
What is this?"

"A second chance at life"

Outside,
the last ships still governed by crew still loyal to Argoss fight back, setting off explosives inside as warriors pour in from all sides, trying to make their escape.
As Leonidas and them come out of the ship, the air outside is littered thick with explosions and rain as ships fall with flames to the ground among warriors parading around with armfuls of loot.

The very last of the able-bodied ships can be seen flying overhead, as some of them have opted to turn and retreat over the hill....
As the ships gradually make their way towards the edge of the hill, bands of warriors run after them laughing, taunting, throwing rocks while some jump, tossing their arms up rapturously.

Chasing the ships past the hill and well beyond the out-stretch of the field, the warriors and their joyful caravan of spirited dance and heckles parade and whoop as they pursue and gradually fade along with the ships as both groups make their way far off into the distance...

The clouds in the sky churn, gray,
thick,
pissed,
awake,
flashing angrily as Leonidas stands at the edge of the hill, looking out from it under the lightning and rain.
KRI-CLASSHHH!!!

Joined by Cerix, Brachias, and several others, Leonidas can't help wonder what lies in store for him next.
"We will rebuild," he utters quietly to himself, looking over towards the fallen city of Draman-TU...
In the spirit of conquest, Leonidas opts to give this planet a new name.
He'll call it Sparta.

And Sparta it shall remain from this day always...

"Things *have* changed.
That much is certain.
But with change comes the timeless spirit of rebirth."

As the day draws to a close,
Leonidas says goodbye to the past,
as he turns,
and walks away,

with his eyes set on the future...

-The End-

THANKS FOR READING!

Obviously Scylus is a little upset, but he'll get over it.

ARGOSS
TWO WEEKS LATER

Inside the dimly lit confines of Lord Melech's chamber, Melech and Scylus go over the events of Draman-TU. Standing with his back facing Scylus, Melech goes over his report while slowly flipping through pages of the Magnus Compendium...

Scylus kneels with his head down, facing the floor.

" I'm ready to accept any punishment for my failure, my lord."

"Hmf...

So the Spartans got away?"

"Yes, my lord."

"And you lost *your* men as well?..."

"Yes, my lord.

They joined up with the Spartans.

I-I tried to take control, b-but by the time I did they were already too far gone in Leonidas's influence."

"I see...

Well, that's no matter."

"Lord?"

"The Spartans will be too busy fending for themselves on Draman-TU.

They'll pose no threat to us anytime soon...

In the meantime, the Etherians have come up with an ingenious new device that promises to offer the solution to your problem with soldiers and... obedience."

"Sir?

I-I don't understand."

"Never mind.

A successor to the Transmutation Matrix is nearing completion and I want you to go back to that little planet you found the Spartans on and fetch me the remains of this...

I'll have everything in order by the time you return..."

Melech holds the Magnus Compendium open towards Scylus's face, where the image of a man on horseback is prominently displayed on a page...

Above the image reads an impressive list of names, dates, and battles won—all credited to this person throughout the course of his lifetime...

And on the bottom page, just below the image, lies a name to which Scylus inadvertently reiterates out loud...

"Alexander The Great?..."

Hey, thanks for checking out the first install-
ment of Spartans In Space.
This book has been a long time coming.
We had to use a lot of underground channels
and outdated methods in order to get this book
made under the noses of all the naysayers.
I'm talking a maze of sewers and tunnels,
dripping pipes, and rushing all the way to the
surface to deliver the book while trying to
avoid the giant rat people that like to munch on
the pages.
It's rough living out here!

Being an underground writer isn't all bad
though.
The sewers aren't crowded, and I live close to
four alien dudes with goo-ish dreads, whose
flesh is green and see-through, and know how
to party.
We usually just hang out at their place and
watch old Bruce Lee flicks when there's
nothing else to do.
Hiya!
Ha-ha!

No, but seriously, thanks for your support.
I'm currently working out the kinks to Spartans
In Space 2: Rise Of Alexander, while roasting
a grilled cheese sandwich over a flaming drum,
hanging out with two mutated lemons with
arms, that talk and have teeth.
They're pretty cool.
A little vile.
But the company's true.

AFTERWORD

A big shout out to Gabo Ibarra, Alfonso Ruiz, Kote Carvajal and Mad Max Bertolini for taking time out from laying art down in their own respective dimensions and coming over to ours to give face to all the characters found throughout the pages of Spartans In Space.

We couldn't have done it without you.

And we couldn't have done it without you! The reader!

It took a lot of guts to do what you did!

Checking out a book you've never heard of, written by an author you know nothing about, and agreeing to go on this journey with me without any idea about how it might end.

Glad to see you're adventurous.

Stay the course...

Welp,

some of the hot cheese fell on top of one of the lemons while I was biting into my sandwich.

He's hopping in pain now, talking crazy cursing up a storm.

Poor little guy.

I got to handle this.

You only make so many friends down here so you got to look after the ones you got.

I'll see you guys around.

And don't forget to check out

Spartans In Space 2: Rise Of Alexander—

if the naysayers don't catch wind of it first,

and the giant rat people don't swipe it to munch on, while climbing up to the surface.

Until then!

END OF BOOK

If you enjoyed this book please leave a positive review on the author's page

amazon.com/author/jaydeehotter

Thank you for supporting local art

Made in the USA
Monee, IL
28 June 2023